A Shoe Addict's
Christmas

Also by Beth Harbison

✳

A Shoe Addict's
Christmas

Beth Harbison

St. Martin's Press
New York

This is a work of fiction. All of the characters, organizations, and events portrayed in this novel are either products of the author's imagination or are used fictitiously.

www.stmartins.com

LIBRARY OF CONGRESS CATALOGING-IN-PUBLICATION DATA

Names: Harbison, Elizabeth M., author.
Title: A shoe addict's Christmas / Beth Harbison.
Description: First edition. | New York : St. Martin's Press, 2016.
Identifiers: LCCN 2016024800| ISBN 9781250087218 (hardcover) |
    ISBN 9781250087232 (e-book)
Subjects: LCSH: Christmas stories. | BISAC: FICTION /
    Contemporary Women. | GSAFD: Ghost stories.
Classification: LCC PS3558.A564 S58 2016 | DDC 813/ .54—dc23
LC record available at https://lccn.loc.gov/2016024800

Our books may be purchased in bulk for promotional, educational, or business use. Please contact your local bookseller or the Macmillan Corporate and Premium Sales Department at 1-800-221-7945, extension 5442, or by e-mail at MacmillanSpecialMarkets@macmillan.com.

First Edition: October 2016

10   9   8   7   6   5   4   3   2   1

To my parents (Jack and Connie McShulskis)
and my children (Paige and Jack Harbison),
who have always made Christmas magical in my life.

Also, in memory of John Harbison,
with whom I shared many magical holidays.

Acknowledgments

Thanks to Tris Zeigler and Lucinda Denton for reading early versions of this manuscript and giving their wonderful feedback.

Thanks to Jack Harbison for the awesome brainstorming, which inspired me so much.

Finally, much gratitude to Jen Enderlin for giving me the chance to write this—I had so much fun!—and to Annelise Robey for cheerleading even through the roughest times.

A Shoe Addict's
Christmas

✳

Chapter 1

It was a picture-perfect Christmas Eve. Snow was falling at almost two inches an hour, swirling down in front of the Simon's Department Store window displays on Massachusetts Avenue like flakes in a snow globe. People either hurried past—clutching their coats to them and closing their eyes against the cold—or ambled along, looking up and around with childlike wonder at the beauty. Even the most ordinary scene, like the Exxon service station across the street from the main door, took on a fairy-tale quality, like a gingerbread house iced in a confection of snow.

Simon's, where I worked in human resources, would have been the perfect subject inside a snow globe, or maybe an impressionistic painting. The owner, Lex Prather, was a very old-fashioned guy (bow tie, martinis, a physique as straight and trim as a cigarette), and I swear he designed the place with Fred Astaire movies in mind.

Or maybe it was more accurate to say that the store was established in the thirties and all of the owners since then, including Lex's late mother and now he himself, had maintained it as the kind of setting where you wouldn't be at all surprised to see a guy in a top hat and tails walk in.

There was even a glove counter. Small, admittedly. Not the most popular department in the store, by any means, but it did more business than you'd expect. There are always Audrey Hepburn/Holly Golightly wannabes, and this was like a Wonderland to them; there are always Women of a Certain Age, and Simon's had everything to make them feel younger, prettier, or happy exactly as they were. Weirdly, a surprising number of dance students also patronized the store. I've never been able to figure out that one, except that we were one of the closest high-end department stores to Georgetown, American University, and George Washington University.

Of all the stuff that was great in Simon's, the shoe department was the best, at least as far as I was concerned. And as far as the readers of *Washingtonian* magazine were concerned as well, since it always rated a mention in the annual roundup. Simon's had begun as a shoe store in the early thirties and had grown rapidly from that, but we still maintained one of the best ranges of sizes in the business. Well, besides online places—hard to compete with Zappos in that arena. But we carried small, handmade brands that the big online companies couldn't.

My friend Lorna Rafferty and her business partners at Shoe Addicts Anonymous were among the best shoe designers around, and we were one of the company's only distributors. Because it had made the gossip columns when it started up—thanks to the dramas of some of the owners—a lot of people came searching for its shoes in particular. Made in Italy from the finest materials, exquisitely designed by a team headed by an unbelievably gorgeous Italian stallion . . . Not that his hot looks were on purpose; he was a brilliant shoe designer, something like fifth generation in a line of shoemakers, but his good looks and charisma were a happy coincidence that got the company even more press.

Everything about its story spoke to a woman's heart.

Of course, there were plenty of plain old shoe addicts themselves at Simon's, looking for any or all brands, and more importantly for the experience of shopping for them there.

The shoe floor was a gorgeous treat of clean lines—up, down, left, right, it was classic upmarket department store all the way. But Lex had gone further and gotten tall, flattering mirrors that were true, not the cheap ones that warped subtly at the belly, putting on an imaginary five pounds. The lighting was soft, too, showcasing the shoes like so many gems. You know how you look at a pair of earrings at the jewelry store and get mesmerized by the sparkle? The Simon's shoe department was like that, only it was the shoes that gleamed and shone under each of the spotlights. At night, with no other lights on, it almost looked like a musical number from one of those old Busby Berkeley movies, each light shining down on some beautiful starlet who might or might not become a star someday.

Each display told a story, and everyone loves to buy a great story.

Here's the one about the wedding!
This one is a wonderful summer evening on the patio.
First date! But I've got a good feeling about this . . .

I read an article once that said that's how women shop—they buy a story, a fantasy. Every item chosen comes with an accompanying narrative in her head. Men tend to be more in and out with a list and no extras.

These were stories I wanted to buy by the armful. It was all I could do to avoid the lure of the shoe department— but I had to, or I'd never be able to make my rent or pay my utilities!

As it was, I worked in human resources, and the hours were long, so I didn't get into the front rooms very often. In fact, tonight was a perfect example of that. I was wrapping up some year-end things, including, thanks to an urgent note from Lex, a fruitless search through storage for the file of an employee named Charlene Pennymar, who'd worked there in the eighties and whom he *had to find*.

Tracking down a long-gone employee was harder than he must have imagined, made even more so because so many people who might remember her had already left for vacations and holiday time off. The entire last week had been filled with excited chatter about skiing in Vail, basking in Martinique, riding and roping in Texas, and chasing exhausted children through the parks in Orlando. It all sounded good from a safe distance, but when Lorna had asked me to accompany her on a trip to Rome, leaving Christmas Day, I balked.

It was another one of those things that I feared would sound good, look good on paper, but end up being more of a challenge than expected. I know that sounds crazy— why do you think I didn't tell many people about the invite?—but when it comes down to it, I'm a real homebody. Typical Cancer on the astrological charts, afraid to leave and, when I did, eager to get back.

Lex, in fact, had tried to persuade me to take a trip between Christmas and New Year's, since it was "the perfect time of year for some R&R by a crackling fire with a hot toddy in hand and a hot man by your side." I wasn't quite sure, though, whether that was his vision for me or for himself.

Anyway, I've never been entirely clear on what a hot toddy is, and as for a hot man by my side? Unless you count feverish, sneezing Doug from bookkeeping, who had come to say good-bye and wish me happy holidays in a cough cloud of germs, I hadn't been around anyone who was a digit over 98.6 in *quite* some time.

As for the other kind of hot—the kind Lex meant— forget it. In my little life there were few surprises.

Anyway, back to Christmas Eve this year. I worked for several hours solid, without looking up or speaking to another person, so finally, just after 7:30 P.M., I reached a stopping point and leaned back for a break. The store closed in half an hour, and if I started hitting a new pile, I probably wouldn't be out until New Year's, so I decided to go grab some dinner at Filigree—the store's fabulous in-house restaurant—and then go home, although honestly I wasn't in that much of a hurry, given that I was going to be alone. I have no siblings, my mom is long gone, and my dad and stepmother, Carla, live in Charleston, S.C., where her family is from.

So, dragging my feet some, I put my work aside and went out to execute the few plans I did have for the night.

But when I went out into the store, I was greeted by . . . nothing. The place was empty. Nat King Cole was crooning faintly from the speakers, that eerie tune about Toyland, and the whole store was as lonely and otherwise silent as a tomb.

I felt like Rip Van Winkle, without the good long rest.

"Hello?" I called foolishly. As if everyone were going to jump out from behind mannequins and display counters and shout, "Surprise!"

Unsurprisingly, there was not a festive peep.

In fact, it was so obvious no one was there that I think I feared an answer more than hoped for one.

Had something gone terribly wrong while I was locked away in my office? Like that episode of *The Twilight Zone* where the bank teller is reading in the bank vault while a bomb wipes everyone out and he emerges into a world where he's alone and then he breaks his glasses?

Creepy things like that are never far from my mind, thanks to watching every episode of *The Twilight Zone, The Outer Limits,* and *Kraft Suspense Theatre* when I was a kid, so I went to the door to check the streets for any sign of life.

I was glad to see the lights were all on out there as usual, but there wasn't a lot of movement. I imagined I could hear the thick silence. Snowflakes twirled around the streetlights before they fell to the ground or blew across the landscape in the modest wind. Somehow in the time since I'd commented on the quaintness of the scene and gone back to the storage room behind my office to search in vain for Charlene Pennymar's file, the snow had really piled up.

Naturally I tried the door. It would be stupid to stand behind it like a lost child, looking at the outside world, and not at least *try* it. But it was locked tight, and the lights above told me that the alarm was on. If worse came to worst, I could always smash a window to get the attention of the police.

I hurried back to my office and took my phone from my purse. A call from Lorna, two from Carla (along with a text that said *MERRY CHRISTMAS EVE* in all caps— I could not get her to understand that was shouting in Textville), and one from a number I didn't recognize. Probably another recording; I'd been getting tons of those calls lately, just a recorded voice, telling me I could pay back my nonexistent student loans at a lower rate (I'd graduated ten years ago with no debt), or that home employment was just a few digits' dialing away. I was at least encouraged to see that I had reception.

First I called Sandy, my co-worker, whom I had last seen this morning over coffee.

"Happy holidays!" she chirped after two rings.

"I'm stuck in the store." God, how Eeyore of me! But what could I do, repeat it with a jolly lilt in my voice?

"What? Hello?"

"Sandy, it's me, Noelle." Yes, *Noelle*. Yes, named for the holiday. I was a July baby; the story was that my father said it was "Christmas in July" when I came along, and my parents had agreed immediately upon the name. "I'm stuck in the store," I said again. Then the obvious question, *"Why is it closed?"*

"Noelle! What do you mean why is the store closed?"

"I mean what happened? I'm stuck in here, alone, and the doors are all locked and alarmed, and I don't know how to get out without creating a huge mess of police and alarm-company employees!" A small surge of hysteria caught in my throat. I stopped and took a deep breath. There was nothing to panic about. I spent more hours here than anywhere else, so what difference did it really make that I was here now?

"But—why are you there? We closed at six!"

"*Why?*"

"Well, look outside, baby girl. The snow is coming down like a thousand inches an hour!"

"And the store closed at *six?*" I took the phone from my ear and looked at the time. It was seven forty. I hadn't missed it by much, but if the snow really was coming down so rapidly, an hour and a half's worth of it had accumulated on top of what they'd decided was too much to stay open an hour and a half ago.

"Lex didn't want anyone out traveling in dangerous weather, especially not on Christmas Eve." Her voice was starting to mirror my anxiety. Or at least boost it. "Honest to Pete, how on earth did you miss that?"

I sighed. How *had* I missed it? Had I gotten that lost in my work? "I was looking for a file for Lex, and I went into the archives and, well, I guess I lost track of time."

"I'll say! What are you going to do? How did you get in to work today?"

"I drove. My car is in the garage."

"Well, *that's* good, at least. It won't get flattened by a salt truck. But still, the roads are a mess. You absolutely cannot go out on them. Not in the car."

I sure couldn't go on foot. My apartment was about five miles away, but five miles in this mess might as well have been a hundred. I tried to picture myself making the walk there on these all-but-abandoned tundra-esque streets, and quickly decided I'd rather just go to the bedding department and sleep in a display. "You're right," I told Sandy. "Not that it matters. I can't even get out of the store."

"What are you going to *do?*" she asked fretfully. "Are you warm enough?"

I laughed. "If you can name me one place that's *more* comfortable than Simon's, I will give you a hundred bucks."

"True." She gave a small laugh. "And the phones and electricity are working?"

"Absolutely. Don't worry about me. I'm just going to give Lex a quick call and let him know what's going on. See if he has any brilliant suggestions. But I don't see how to fight Mother Nature, so I'll probably just hang out here for the night and leave in the morning when they dig the streets out."

"That's always about four A.M.," Sandy commented. "They scrape along the street, and Bill thinks they're going to hit the cars every time."

"There aren't a lot of cars out now, that's for sure. So don't worry, I'll be fine."

"Call me if you need anything. *Anything.*"

And what could she do? But I didn't ask that. Sandy was a mother and more prone to worry than most. Even more than me. "I will," I said, and we hung up.

Next I dialed Lex. He answered just when I was about to give up, and sounded as if he had a good couple of hours of celebration under his belt already. I imagined his apartment, glowing with real candles, a tree alight with heavy tin tinsel, a martini in every guest's hand. I hated to interrupt with a problem, but I didn't see an alternative.

I explained the situation to him.

"I'll send the fire department immediately," he declared, ever dramatic.

"No!" I could well imagine what that would look like, wasting the city's resources on one dumb woman who had managed to get herself stuck in a high-end store with every luxury amenity anyone could dream of and few could afford. "I'm going to hunker down here," I told him. "I just wanted to let you know the situation in case anyone is monitoring the cameras or whatever."

"That's usually handled by Bulldog, the overnight security guard, but he called in with a fake stomach flu earlier, so there's no one."

It hadn't occurred to me to wonder where the overnight security guard was, and now that I knew he'd called in and wouldn't be here, a tremor of discomfort shivered down my spine. I was well and truly alone.

But I didn't want to worry Lex, especially since it was painfully clear that there were far worse places to be trapped, in the snow, on Christmas Eve, or otherwise. Honestly, this was better than being stuck at the Four Seasons in Manhattan.

"If you get hungry, you make sure you go on over to Filigree and help yourself to whatever you like," Lex was saying, then corrected himself. "Not *if* you get hungry, *when* you get hungry."

"I don't want to upset Gemma's inventory."

"Nonsense. She'd be horrified to even hear you say that! I want you to make yourself *absolutely* at home. Don't you worry about a thing. As long as you're safe inside there, I'm not going to worry. Heaven knows you're as safe as you'd be locked in a fortress."

And that was basically the situation. I was locked in a fortress. Alone. Actually, it was kind of a fantasy come true.

Lex and I hung up, and I looked around. Locked in a beautiful fortress. What did I want to do? I had the entire store to myself. What was first?

Clothes.

The funny thing about working at Simon's was that my hours were often so long that I didn't get many chances to shop. This was, if nothing else, a great opportunity to pick up a few much-needed items. In fact, it was a great opportunity to take advantage of the Christmas sale *and* my employee discount.

My phone rang. I looked at it.

Gemma.

"Like you didn't do this on purpose," she joked the minute I answered. "Forget men and tight abs and champagne; every woman's *real* fantasy is to get locked in a department store overnight."

I had to laugh. "I'm trying to look at it that way, but, boy, the place feels really different when no one is here."

In the background a baby screamed. Gemma sighed.

"Paul is getting the baby overexcited, and we're going to be up all night long with him."

"With Paul or the baby?"

"Paul, of course." She laughed. "He cannot wait to have a first Christmas to beat the band. Anyway, Lex told me you were making noise about worrying about eating my food, but I've got to tell you I have baby-mama brain and haven't been ordering as well as I should. If you can eat some of that stuff, you'd actually be doing me a favor. Especially the cheese. I got carried away thinking about cheese plates and went a little nuts. Oh! There are spiced nuts, too. To go with the cheese. Trust me, they're amazing. And top the Brie with some of the balsamic cherries in the flat white container in the fridge."

"Thanks, Gemma."

"Will you be okay? Do you need me to come up with a few simple recipes? I think everything should be easy for you to find."

"I'll be *fine*," I told her. "Honest. And I'll eat some cheese."

"Good! And sorbet! There's fresh raspberry sorbet in

the freezer. I got a lot of that after trying a sample in Chelsea Market."

"Sounds fabulous." And it did. "Now go Christmas Eve-ing with your family and don't worry about me."

"Okay." She sounded doubtful. "If you're sure you don't need anything else from me."

"Honestly? I need you to let me go so I can do some shopping." The truth was, it was comforting to hear her voice, but I didn't want her wasting her night on me.

Plus, I knew she'd understand that shopping thing. "Well, then! Go to it! Have a blast."

I thanked her and told her I would. Then I told myself the same, because this was no time to feel trapped or sorry for myself.

So I spent a good forty-five minutes trying on clothes in a scene that looked like the ones from so many chick flicks. Only I didn't have a best friend or love interest there, goading me along and clapping with approval at every look that worked or was hilarious. And, believe me, I had both. Let's just say caftans are not my style, and I don't know what yacht I thought I was going to be sitting on, eating berries with mimosas for breakfast, wearing one.

I did, however, find a bunch of things I *did* want, and I made a pile and left it on the counter.

Then I went to the bedding department to choose my bed for the night. Sounds ridiculous, I know, but I was really pretty psyched about that part. My bed at home sagged in the middle, and I spent every night feeling like I was trying to crawl up a ravine, but so far I'd just been too lazy to get a new mattress. If I got a new mattress, I'd want a bigger one, which meant a new frame, which meant me disassembling the one I had, and—ugh. It was just more than I felt like dealing with, so I stuck with the same old bed for now.

The beds at Simon's, though . . . wow. Top end.

"Who's been sleepin' in my bed?" I asked no one, as I threw back the thousand-dollar Belgian linen sheets on Bed Number One. God, they were luxurious. I didn't know how rich I'd have to be in order to justify such a purchase without thinking about the hundreds of other necessities I might have gotten with the same money, but I sure wasn't there now.

The only problem with the bed was that it was kind of out in the open. Granted, no one else was in the store, and I knew it, but I also knew I'd feel vulnerable trying to sleep there.

So I went to another bed, this one bordered by a wall and topped with rose-gold silk sheets. They were almost as expensive as the linen, truth be told, and the latest sales angle was that silk kept your skin from wrinkling and kept your hair smooth. Well, who wouldn't want that?

I got in the bed for a moment and reveled in the luxury. "And this one was *just right.*" Thank goodness the security guard *wasn't* there, because if he'd come upon me, I would have sounded like a lunatic. But I was having fun. What the heck, right?

I left the bed turned down, half wishing some magic housekeeper had left a chocolate on my pillow. This was about as close as I was going to get to staying in a four-star hotel, and I wanted to enjoy every minute.

I smiled to myself. This really was fun. Another person might have freaked out at being trapped—hell, another *me* might have freaked out at being trapped—but with the cheerful holiday music playing (it was Andy Williams and "It's the Most Wonderful Time of the Year" right now), it was hard to feel anything but festive.

Next up was the lingerie department. I needed a nightgown and robe. Well, *needed* . . . maybe I didn't *need* them, but I couldn't see myself sleeping comfortably if I just stripped down to my undies, and I sure couldn't see myself walking around in this potential fishbowl in a T-shirt, in case the roads cleared and the world came back to life.

Besides, I didn't actually *have* a nice nightgown and robe (see "T-shirt" above—that's what I usually sleep in). It seemed like a good idea to have at least one in case I ever had company or, God willing, any sort of romantic life. So I picked them out and went into the dressing room to change.

Did I mention this was fun?

It was *really* fun.

I took the tags off and added them to my pile of clothes at the casuals department cash register.

"The Christmas Waltz" came on, and I began dancing goofily to it, sweeping past the window with its view of the snowy outside, and feeling lighter and happier than

I could remember feeling in a long, long time. *This* was it—*this* was the "holiday spirit" everyone talked about. I'd been meh about it for so long, year after year, but at this moment, it didn't matter that I was alone and that I didn't have any big plans for tomorrow; all that mattered was that I was in a magical place, and for the rest of my life no one would ever be able to ruin this moment or take it away from me.

That's when it happened.

There was a tremendously loud crash in the shoe department, about fifteen yards away, past Men's Suits and Juniors. Not a "Hm, something fell off the wall, that's strange, it must not have been on very securely" crash, but more of a "Good lord, the wall must have just caved in!" crash.

Then a shrill, worried exclamation. I'm pretty sure it was "Zooterkins!"

I was not alone.

Chapter 2

I stopped dead in my tracks and listened, like a twitchy doe, for one more hint that I should run for the hills. Only there were no hills, even on a good day when the doors would open, and running could only take me as far as a corner to be, well, *cornered* in.

My mind raced. *Zooterkins.* It was hardly a menacing word. And the voice that had uttered it had been . . . fussy? Female for sure, now that I thought about it. But not tough New Jersey *Mob Wives* female, more like an elementary school teacher. My grandmother. Anyone's grandmother.

But what was I to do? I mean, I was barefoot, in a satin nightgown and robe, miles from my phone, and the only thing I could use as a weapon, if need be, would be a stiletto.

Which wasn't a bad idea. I grabbed a Ferragamo spike-heel pump from the display table and headed toward the back room of the shoe department, where the noise had come from. Once I got as far as the counter, I could pick up the phone there. It was better than a mobile because the minute I hit 911, emergency crews would be on the way. Assuming they had sled dogs. But I couldn't afford to think about what could go wrong.

I moved as stealthily as possible. Interesting side note: Satin makes a whole lot of noise when you are otherwise in silence and want to remain that way. Still, I made it to the phone and picked it up. So, with phone in one hand and shoe in the other, I stood at the door to the back room and called, "Hello?"

Pause. "Oh, hello."

It sounded like an old woman—but so stereotypically like an old woman that I could picture it being a big, burly man with a gift for mimicry.

"I have the police on the line," I said, then hit the CALL button to be sure I had a line out. I did; it hummed so loud I had to hit the button again to turn it off. "They're on the way."

"Oh, dear." There was an unidentifiable bustling sound. "This isn't how this was supposed to go at all."

If that wasn't genuinely an old woman, it was a *damn* good imitation. I relaxed fractionally.

"I'm sorry?" I asked. "How *what* was supposed to go?"

Worried sounds came as an answer, then, "I've blown it. Just like last time."

I had no idea what to do with this. "Um . . . ma'am? Can you please come out here?" Then what? What would I do?

"I could, dear, but who would clean up this mess?"

"Mess?" I remembered the sound that had brought me in this direction and took a tentative step in. "What mess? What on earth happened?"

Then I saw. There were shoes all over the floor, mismatched pairs lying haphazardly. The huge metal shelf that had held them was leaning against the wall opposite where it usually stood, at an angle forming a virtual steeple over what looked, indeed, like an elderly woman in a high-necked dress and the kind of boots Mary Poppins wore. Her white hair was an unkempt bun, leaving tendrils of pale gray to frame her moonlike face. She looked like the kind of person who smiled frequently, but she wasn't smiling now.

She was looking downright fretful. Cartoonishly so.

"What happened?" I asked again, setting both the phone and the shoe down and going in to assess the damage.

"My hat," she said, indicating the floor a few feet away, where a small pile of pink fabric sat with a feather poking out of it, askew. It was surrounded by shoes. "When I came in"—she gestured vaguely upward—"it got knocked off on the top of the shelf, and I was going back up to get it. Climbing up, you see, because I just don't *present* as well without it." She sighed and knitted her brow, looking around at the wreckage. "You can see exactly what happened."

"Are you saying," I began, unable to believe it. Surely she wasn't. Or was she? "That you were *climbing the shelves* to try to retrieve your hat?"

She hesitated, then nodded. "Of course, I realize that sounds silly now."

"It sounds insane."

"Oh, Zooterkins, I know it does." She looked at me plaintively. "I don't have a better explanation than the truth, though, do I?"

"Okay . . ." Lord, the mess. I was *not* in the mood to deal with a batty old lady and two thousand mismatched shoes. Five minutes ago I was freaked out at the idea of being alone here; now I was freaked out at the idea of *not* being alone.

It felt like I was supposed to be tested this Christmas Eve one way or the other, and I'd taken being locked in too much in stride, so God or Santa Claus or *whoever* had thrown something else my way.

"Who are you?" I asked her. Someone must be waiting for her, worried about her. Some grandchild, maybe, or even an old man sitting outside in an ancient rear-wheel-drive Cadillac that was getting increasingly buried in snow.

"Oh! That! That's easy. I'm your guardian angel!"

Oh boy. My guardian angel. This was obviously a fan of holiday movies. "Is anyone waiting for you? Expecting you? Should we make a call?"

"Only one way to make a call to my boss." She widened her eyes, pointing upward, then put her hands together as if in prayer. When she smiled, it made her round apple cheeks go red and her watery blue eyes damn near twinkle.

This was immediately tiresome, not because it wasn't charming—it was—but because it wasn't *true,* and the truth needed to be discovered because there were probably some people out there worried to death about her.

"What's your name?" I tried.

"Call me Charlie."

Great. "Okay. I'm Noelle—"

"Oh, I know that. Christmas in July, wasn't it?"

"Yes," I answered automatically, then realized that wasn't something a stranger should know.

"I learn that sort of thing before taking on a job," she explained. "It helps me prove to you I'm telling the truth."

I wasn't sure what it proved besides that she was an exceptionally lucky guesser. Exceptionally. But that was hard to buy. A good guess would have been that I was born at Christmas, or that it was my mother's favorite holiday, neither of which was the truth. I supposed "Christmas in July" was guessable—it *is* an expression, after all—but still . . .

"Don't worry, dear," she said. "Goodness, you look so fretful. It's difficult to strike the right balance between reassuring someone and alarming them. I apologize if I've alarmed you."

Now she just sounded like an old lady again. Absolutely typical, nothing scary. It was easy to let go of the uncomfortable question of how she knew the origin of my name and to return to the idea that she needed to be accounted for somehow.

"What's your last name?" I asked her.

She shrugged, not a care in the world. "Don't remember. Must have had one once, but I don't anymore. I'm just known as Charlie around the clouds, so that's what you can call me. Unless you want me to make up a last name. I can do that."

"All right, why don't you?" Chances seemed decent that she might "make up" her own real last name and I could call Lex or Sandy or someone to have them figure this out.

"Let's see . . " She tapped her finger against her chin, then looked at me and raised an eyebrow. "Smith?"

I shook my head.

"Jones."

"Nope."

"Moneypenny!"

"That's from James Bond."

"Oh, but it's such a fine last name. All shiny and coppery. I do love it."

I sighed.

"Carpenter."

"That's *my* last name."

"I know, dear. You see?" She tapped a pudgy index finger against her temple. "I did it again, slipped it right in there."

"How do you know my name?" Then it occurred to me—the company newsletter. Maybe she was a relative of someone who worked at Simon's, which would explain why she was here, and she'd seen my picture and maybe even heard a story from someone I'd had an unlikely conversation with.

"I really think we should contact your family to let them know that you're all right."

She looked bereft for a moment, then said, "I don't have family here."

"In town?"

"On earth."

It was obvious I wasn't going to get anywhere with this line of questioning, so I gave up. "Fine. I'll call you Charlie, and we'll forget the last name for the moment."

"Excellent. Noelle."

I looked again at the shoes. What a mess. It was going to be a long night. "Do you want to try to help me put these back, Charlie?"

"Of course! I'm the reason for the mess, after all." She bustled over to the pink hat and set it crookedly atop her head, then gave me a nod as if to say, *Now I'm ready to work!*

"So first let's just match up shoe styles, then size, then find the boxes, how does that sound?"

"Like I've created a heck of a mess."

"You have." I laughed. "But we're going to fix that."

We set about collecting styles and pairs, which wasn't as bad as it had seemed like it would be, since of course everything had fallen straight off the shelves and onto the floor in front of where it had been. It wasn't as if shoes had ended up thirty feet away from each other.

"So what do you do for work?" I asked Charlie casually.

"Angel," she said. "Not a very good one." She was focused on picking up shoes, with not a hint of self-consciousness in her voice or facial expression. "I'm working on guardian angel." She glanced at me. "You're my first. They always give the klutzes like me to the nice ones like you."

I was momentarily flattered until I remembered that what she was saying was nuts. "What did you do before that?"

"I can't say I remember."

"You can't remember?"

"My life here, on earth. That's what you're asking, isn't it?"

"I guess so." This was too weird.

"I don't remember it. I did once, but I've been gone a long, long time. At least by your standards."

The idea of that being true—though I totally wasn't believing it—struck me as inestimably sad. A whole life forgotten?

"Oh, it was a long time ago," she said, as if reading my mind. "I'm surrounded by my loved ones now; it's just that no one can remember who was what." She chuckled heartily. "Now and again, I have had the feeling I was a seamstress, though."

"Yeah?"

"Or a cook." She shrugged. "I'm very picky about both. The hem on this dress"—she gestured—"it just makes me bonkers. The stitches are too big, too loopy, and so the hem isn't right."

I looked at her hem, but nothing was obviously shoddy.

"Then again . . ." She sighed. "I do love to eat. I haven't eaten in ages. Absolute ages."

I hadn't either, come to think of it, and I remembered Gemma's description of the cheeses in the kitchen. "Want to go grab a bite in the restaurant?" I asked her.

"What? Is it open?"

I laughed. "Well, no. The entire store is closed. Which is why I was so surprised that you're here." I felt like I should ask again if anyone was looking for her, but, honestly, she seemed a lot more like some poor soul who had gotten stuck and wanted to make a good story of it than a kook who didn't know who or where she was. She was going a bit heavy on the guardian-angel bit, which made me think she'd probably watched a few too many Christmas movies and found the perfect way to occupy herself on an otherwise-lonely Christmas Eve.

She was certainly occupying me. I have to confess, I was kind of enjoying playing out my little Christmas story.

"Let's go grab a bite, then come back and finish up here."

"Very well," she said, following my lead as I walked out into the brightly lit store. "Is my hat okay?" she asked.

I turned and looked at her. What had been a pink blob on the floor, with a crooked feather, was now a pink blob on her head, with a crooked feather. "It's perfect," I told her.

We made our way to Filigree, a little Mary Poppins/ Cherry Tree Lane of a spot, with twisted white wrought-iron gates and delicate tables and chairs, and a commercial kitchen that was equipped to cook for a legitimate army.

I, however, was *not* fit to cook for an army. I was used to cooking, rather poorly, for myself. My repertoire was quite limited. "Do you like cheese?" Everyone likes cheese, right?

She shook her head. "No, dear. Makes me gassy, I'm afraid."

"Egg and toast?" I offered.

"That sounds *lovely.*"

"Excellent." I took out a couple of plates, found a few slices of bread, plus butter and eggs from the fridge, and took a pan down from the rack and put it on the stove to heat. My mother used to call these Bull's-eye Eggs. I buttered the bread and placed it buttered side down in the pan. "So what makes you think you're a guardian angel?"

"They said you'd be like this."

"Who said I'd be like what?"

"Not just you," she hastened to correct. "They said everyone is like this. I imagine I would have been, too. Or was." She drifted off into thought for a moment, and I watched her. "I just don't know."

"I'm sorry," I said. "You lost me."

"Oh! Oh! Yes indeed. They, the crew above, they said that no one ever believes anymore. That everyone is skeptical and thinks they're dealing with a loon." She narrowed her eyes and looked at me. "Do you think you're dealing with a loon?"

"I don't know," I said honestly. "But I don't think I'm dealing with a guardian angel."

She seemed to consider that, then gave a nod of acceptance. "That's fair."

"No offense, of course."

"None taken, I assure you."

I took out a small glass and cut a hole into each piece of toast with it, then cracked an egg into each and topped them with salt and pepper. As I watched the egg grow white around the edges, I asked, "If you're a guardian angel sent to me on purpose, why?"

"Because this is the time of year you reflect the most and feel the worst," she answered simply.

An easy guess, though. I mean, you can't swing a cat by the tail without hitting someone who hates the holidays.

"I don't hate the holidays," I said, without a lot of conviction.

"I didn't say you did. *You* said that."

"Okay, I don't feel the worst during the holidays."

She raised an eyebrow.

"I hate the holidays." I flipped the eggs and put the circle I'd cut out of them back over the yolks in the center. "I do, I hate the holidays. There, I said it." After a few seconds, I scooped an egg-and-toast onto each plate and took them over to the table where Charlie was sitting. She'd already opened our wrapped silverware. "Hot sauce? Ketchup?" I asked, ready to retrieve them.

"We're getting there," she said, and I realized she thought I'd said *catch up*.

"No, I mean, do you want ketchup or hot sauce? For your eggs?"

She looked at me, utterly puzzled.

So I added, "Or are they fine like this?"

"This is fine," she agreed, then delicately cut a piece of bread off with her knife and fork. She popped it into her mouth and said, "Mmmmmmm. It's been so long."

There was no way to know whether she meant it felt like a long time since lunch or if she hadn't eaten since her mortal days who-knows-how-many-years-ago, though I was pretty sure if I asked her she would answer that it was the latter. So I just said, "Bon appétit."

We ate in silence for a few minutes, but it was nice. How often does a person have a chance like this, to eat in a favorite restaurant virtually alone? Admittedly it would have been better if Gemma had been in the kitchen making some of her fabulous concoctions, but this was pretty ideal as it was, especially since the one of us who did *not* get gassy from cheese went and made a plate of creamy Brie with balsamic cherries, sweet and tart Gorgonzola Dolce, hard aged Parmesan with crystals of flavor in every flake, and a rich Morbier with its vein of ash running through the middle.

Overhead, the Cocteau Twins started singing "Frosty the Snowman" on the never-ending loop of holiday music that played over the system, and my spirits soared.

"Anyway," Charlie went on, "I'm here to help you get over your troubles."

"But I'm not troubled!"

"Does it bother you that you're stuck at work here on a beautiful Christmas Eve?"

"No!"

"Not even when the rest of the world is warm and cozy

in their homes with their families, watching the snow come down, sitting by a crackling fire, maybe singing around a piano or lighting candles or doing whatever rituals each of them has?"

"Does that make me feel bad? No, of course not."

She leaned fractionally forward. "Do you ever wish you had your own traditions and routines on this day?"

"I've never even thought about it."

"There you go. That's trouble." She jabbed her fork at me for emphasis. "Most people want to be with family and friends today, but you're just fine being locked in a retail establishment where you toil forty or more hours every week."

"I love my work!"

"That's all very well and good, missy, but you also love avoiding life."

My ire raised, even while I knew there was an uncomfortable level of truth to what she was saying. "That's not true."

She took the last bite of her egg, looked at my empty plate, and shrugged. "If it weren't true, then you wouldn't need me. And, believe you me, you do. I believe you should have had a visit a long, long time ago. But, of course, I wasn't ready then. Zooterkins, they gave me a tough case to begin with, didn't they?"

I sighed. "Maybe you don't need to try, then?"

She shook her head, essentially pooh-poohing me. "Let's go back and clean up the shoes. I have the most marvelous idea."

Chapter 3

"Pick a pair," she told me, gesturing at the mess that she herself had created. "We're going on a trip. Where do you want to go?"

"We're not going anywhere. There are three feet of snow out there."

"So these." She picked up a pair of Hunter boots in a bright canary yellow. I loved them. I always loved Hunter boots. They reminded me of the snow boots I'd had when I was a little kid. My mother used to call them my Christopher Robin boots. I'd been meaning to buy a pair for ages, but somehow I always ended up talking myself out of it for one reason or another.

This time I took the boots she handed over. My thought

was that the snow that was coming down now was going to be around for quite a while, so even though part of me didn't want to play along with her little game, the other part of me recognized that this was a task well past due. I needed snow boots. Here they were.

In my exact size, even.

"Go on, chicken, try them on," Charlie urged.

I took them in my hands, the sturdy, shiny rubber so much like a new toy that I felt like a kid again just holding them. "I do need some snow boots . . ."

"Of course you do!"

I sat down and put them on, one slow slide at a time. I felt a little dizzy as I did it, but didn't think much of it until they were on and suddenly I wasn't in the shoe department, or the store, anymore.

I was in the family room of my childhood home.

"Tell me what you see." Charlie's voice came from far away. "Tell me what you feel. Tell me everything."

✳

It was Christmas Eve. The worst Christmas Eve there could ever be. The fact that God even let Christmas come at all made Noelle angry. There should never be another Christmas, ever.

Christmas had been her mother's favorite holiday. Her own, too. Once. But not anymore. Not since her mother had *passed* two months ago, in the middle of a hot October.

That's what everyone said: *passed.* She'd *passed.* But Noelle knew she hadn't *passed,* like she'd walked through one room into the next. She'd died. And now she was dead and she was never coming back and everything was wrong and there was no making it right, no matter how much her father might want her to just stop crying and pretend to have a good time.

For one thing, the tinsel was put on the tree in big hunks, not single strands laid over the branches the way Mom had done it. Branches—it was a fake tree anyway, so they weren't even branches. Protrusions. Noelle was a month past twelve and fairly sure that was the right word. Her father and aunt had also just clumped all the decorations on the front, without regard for sizes. If Noelle had helped, as they'd asked her to, she would have known that her mother said the biggest ornaments went on the bottom and got progressively smaller as you moved up to the top of the tree.

Why didn't Aunt Beanie know that? She was Mom's sister! Weren't they raised the same? Whatever. The tree looked stupid, like something out of someone else's house, not her own.

"Cookies?" her father offered awkwardly, bringing in a plate of premade cookies he'd bought from Giant.

"No, thank you," Noelle said.

"Do you . . . do you want to leave some out for Santa?"

"I already know, Dad. I know there's no Santa."

"But last year we—"

"Last year I didn't know. I still believed the lies." She leveled her gaze at him. "I don't believe lies anymore." Lies like *it's for the best,* or *she's out of pain now,* or *she's with you in your heart all the time now,* or *someday you'll see her again.*

People told a lot of lies to try to stop the sadness, but it didn't work.

"What do you want to do, then?"

She took a breath and looked around. Nothing was the

way it had ever been on Christmas before—Couldn't he
see that? Had he never noticed everything her mother
had done?—but it *was* still the same house. She could at
least *try* to have a good time.

Something inside of her, though, something bitter
and angry, wouldn't let her even try.

"I know one thing we should do," Aunt Beanie an-
nounced from the front hall. She stomped the snow off
her feet and instructed her kids—fourteen-year-old Aaron
and bitchy thirteen-year-old Rachel—to do the same.
"Where's the CD player?" she asked, then spotted it on
the hearth next to the fireplace. "Every year when Lynnie
and I were kids, we'd play Bing Crosby singing 'Do
You Hear What I Hear?' on Christmas Eve. Did your mom
do that with you, Noelle?"

She nodded. "Yes." A lump formed in her throat. But
she didn't want to cry. Especially not in front of Aaron
and Rachel.

"Perfect!"

Beanie's enthusiasm was so broad it had to be faked.
No one could be that happy on the first Christmas after

her sister's death. But she was doing it for Noelle, and Noelle knew it and was grateful, even though she secretly just wanted to go to her room and cry until the stupid holiday was over.

The music came on, and everyone chatted away, holiday talk, gift talk, the idea of Beanie and her family maybe taking Noelle on a ski trip they were planning for the New Year's school vacation. She didn't want to go. She didn't want to do anything. She didn't want anyone to expect anything of her right now.

The music played on, and everyone moved into the dining room for a game of Monopoly. Despite herself, Noelle found herself having fun, but as soon as Aunt Beanie asked if she wanted to go stay at her house for the night, she shut down. No, she didn't want to leave home on Christmas Eve. Somehow the very idea made her feel even farther away from her mother. As if she could somehow come back tonight and visit. It was as likely as Santa Claus, maybe even less so, but Noelle wasn't going anywhere.

"Are you sure?" Beanie asked. "It's going to be really fun. The kids are going to stay up all night and watch old holiday movies. I'm going to try, but I always fall asleep before Jimmy Stewart ever meets Clarence." Behind her Rachel nodded, her lank, coffee-colored hair swinging in front of her coffee-colored eyes—for her, a display of wild enthusiasm.

"Why don't you come?" Aaron urged. He actually smiled, showing his full set of braces; the steely teeth and his troubled skin made an unfortunate combination, yet the smile warmed her heart. "We'll make sure you have a good time."

"Yeah," Rachel agreed, though her persuasion ended there. She pushed her limp hair back, and it fell right back in her face.

"We got a toboggan for Christmas Eve," Aaron went on. "We can go ride it down the hill by the middle school."

"No thanks," Noelle said. "I'm just going to go to bed. I'm really tired."

Her aunt and father exchanged a look, and he gave a small shrug. "I'll tuck you in, baby," he said to her.

"No, that's all right. I'm fine. Really." Even to her own

ears she didn't sound convincing. She got up from the sofa and halted at the door to the room. "Thanks, everyone. I'm sorry I'm not so much fun. Merry Christmas." She barely got the last word out before her voice cracked, and she ran upstairs, whipped her door closed behind her, and threw herself onto her bed, crying into her pillow until finally she fell into a hard sleep.

That was where the memory ended. Normally.

But just as she was expecting to explain to Charlie why she'd been so sour as a child that year, the memory started over, only, like a movie, it was something she'd never seen before.

"Why don't you come?" Aaron said. "We'll make sure you have a good time."

"Yeah," Rachel agreed.

"We got a toboggan for Christmas Eve. We can go ride it down the hill by the middle school."

It was on the tip of her tongue to say no. In fact, to tell them all they were being insensitive and downright mean. Didn't they realize she'd lost her mother? That nothing could ever make her happy again? That it was easy for them, with their parents and their nice big house in Potomac Falls, with a pool in the summer and a *toboggan* in winter, but all she had was a fake tree with clumps of tinsel and relatives who were going to get tired of her sadness and mopiness sooner rather than later and she would end up, inevitably, alone.

It took her only a fraction of a second to have all of those thoughts and feelings and then just a fraction of a second more to refuse to fall into that sad, sorry pit. No, she didn't want to go. She wanted to go to her room and cry. But she had the rest of her life to go off by herself and cry whenever she wanted. If she stayed here now, it was absolutely sure to be a miserable Christmas Eve. There was literally no way for her father, or even for her, to get it right when they were both heartbroken and knew everything was so wrong.

So why not try something a little outside her comfort zone? Why not *socialize* a little, instead of moping?

That's what her mom would tell her to do, after all.

She had always told her to get out more, to join in more. Not to be so shy.

So she would. This time she would.

Aunt Beanie's house was a festival of twinkling lights and decorations. She'd gone all out, and Noelle wondered why they'd even bothered to come to her own house at all, with its sad excuse for festivities.

"Noelle Carpenter, where are your snow boots?" Aunt Beanie demanded as the kids were getting ready to go out the front door with their sleds and toboggan.

"I don't have any," Noelle answered. Then, aware that it sounded like they were too poor to afford shoes, she added, "My dad and I were going to go out and get some, but you know how it never snows here. Until now."

Beanie looked out the door at the still-falling snow and made a *hmmph* sound. "Your mother would never have let you go short on shoes! Well, I have just the thing," she said, and opened the hall closet, producing some muddy old yellow rubber Wellington boots. "These were your mom's, but she ordered them a half size too small and ended up giving them to me. Said they were blistering her feet even though she loved them and wore them anyway for a while. She said they reminded her of Paddington Bear. Or was it Christopher Robin? I have a feeling they'll fit you just perfectly with a few pairs of socks. Rachel! Get some socks for Noelle!"

Rachel ran upstairs and came back with two pairs of

thick socks. Noelle wrestled into them and then slid the boots on. "They're perfect!" she breathed. "Well, a little big, but perfect anyway."

"Your mom loved them. It just killed her for me to dance around in them in front of her, but they didn't make her size." Beanie gave a laugh and looked off into the distance, then brought herself back. "Oh, I'm sorry. I didn't mean . . . It didn't *kill* her, obviously." She kneaded her hands in front of her stomach. "I'm so sorry, that seems so insensitive."

"It's okay. She was your sister, you had jokes together. I know you loved her, too. She wouldn't want us to watch every word we say." Noelle tried to think of her own example to make Beanie feel better. "I used to eat ice cream in front of her because she was so afraid of getting fat. Not that she was anything close to it."

"No, she had a great figure."

Until the end, neither of them said. But they both paused, presumably remembering the way cancer and chemo had robbed her of her hair, her appetite, and her strength.

"Anyway"—Beanie clapped her hands together—"*now*

you are ready for the snow. Have fun, little kiddles! And be good! Aaron, Rachel, keep a good eye on your cousin."

Forty-five minutes later, Noelle and Aaron and Rachel were under an inky black sky, dotted with shining stars, ambient light streaming from the basketball and tennis courts, screaming with laughter as they—along with what seemed like the entire student body of Potomac Middle School—whooshed down the hill and across what was normally a wide basketball court but was now a sheet of ice.

"Jacob Marsden keeps looking at you," Rachel said to Noelle on a white puff of breath.

"Who?"

"What do you mean who? The cutest boy in school. Duh."

An unfamiliar thrill ran down Noelle's core. "I don't know who he is, and anyway I'm not old enough to date."

"You're old enough to kiss, and that's just exactly what he wants to do." Rachel's lower lip stuck out involuntarily. "I can't believe you don't even know who he is. Do you know how many girls here have the hots for him?"

"No."

"Plenty."

And suddenly Noelle knew that Rachel was one of them. "Well, I can't do anything about it, so he's all yours." Still, the idea of this boy, whoever and wherever he was, wanting to kiss her was absolutely enthralling. Her heart pounded at the very thought of this mystery boy.

"You'll know who he is soon enough," Rachel promised. "Just pay a little attention to something other than the floor and the tops of your shoes when school starts up again."

Reflexively, Noelle looked down. The smell of snow and ice filled her nostrils.

"Hey!" Aaron ran up to them. "We're going to play Red Rover on the ice, you guys in?"

"Yeah!" Rachel enthused, Jacob Marsden apparently forgotten as quickly as he'd been brought up.

Noelle wasn't sure about this. Seemed like the perfect way to get hurt. But she didn't want to be the party pooper or, worse, the one lone sad girl sitting on the sidelines. "Sure."

Everyone lined up in two lines on either side of the icy basketball court. There was a great deal of negotiation—people being traded back and forth, complaints being registered that there were too many big people on one side and/or too many weaklings on the other.

Eventually Noelle found herself holding hands with a boy she'd never met. She suspected she knew who it was, though, before he even introduced himself.

"You Aaron Neely's cousin?" he asked in a cloud of icy breath.

She stood up taller. "Yes."

"I'm Jacob Marsden. I've seen you in the halls."

"I'm Noelle."

"I know."

Her face felt hot, and she was glad he couldn't see her blush.

"What grade are you in?"

She wanted to lie, but she'd get caught immediately. "Seventh," she said, then added unnecessarily, "Almost eighth."

He nodded as if considering. "I'm in eighth."

"Huh." What else was she supposed to say? Besides, of course, repeating, *Yeah, I'm about to be.* As if she might catch up to him and not be forever one grade behind.

The game started and was so much fun that Noelle was completely lost in it. Every time someone slid through the line, everyone laughed and laughed. Off in the distance there was the sound of carolers walking through the neighborhood. Some were distinctly off-key—maybe the distance made it sound more pronounced—but somehow that just added to the charm of it.

The game went on and on, one breathless rush after another, and pretty quickly Noelle stopped thinking about what night it was beyond one of the most magical nights of her life.

And then, just when she thought it couldn't have gotten any better, when a runner broke through Noelle's grip on Rachel's hand, Jacob took the opportunity to let go of the girl on his other side and run off the basketball court with Noelle. There were enough people still sledding that no one seemed to notice except for Rachel, who gave a lingering look behind her before resuming the game.

"So, Noelle," Jacob said, his voice a little wavery either from the cold or from nerves. "Want to be my girlfriend?"

"I . . . I don't know. What does it mean?"

"You know what it means."

She did. Of course she did. It meant nothing. It meant that they told everyone that they were boyfriend and girlfriend but never saw each other outside of school anyway. It was kind of a lame version of boyfriend and girlfriend, but the whole idea thrilled her, and she wished, more than anything, that she could run home and tell her mother about it.

But her mother would know already. That's what everyone said. That she was with Noelle now and always.

"Sure," she told him.

"Great." He leaned forward and gave her a kiss right on the lips. Just a peck, but still her first kiss. Her heart thrummed nearly out of her chest with excitement. "It's official."

"Okay."

They stood there awkwardly facing each other for a moment, neither knowing what to do next, until someone called Jacob back to the Red Rover game. "Gotta go," he said, and ran back over to his friends.

It was all she could do not to just twirl and twirl and twirl with joy.

Soon parents began to show up, ushering their kids back home. Aunt Beanie was one of them, but she brought Thermoses of piping-hot cinnamon apple cider. Noelle wrapped her hands around the steaming cup and took a sip of the sweet liquid. It warmed her all the way through.

"Did you have fun?" Aunt Beanie asked her, looking concerned.

Noelle felt Rachel's eyes on her. "Oh, yes. Thank you so much for inviting me."

"We're delighted to have you! Let's make it a new tradition. Christmas Eve at our place!"

"Sounds good to me," Noelle said, hoping every year would bring as much fun as this one unexpectedly had.

"You see," Beanie said, taking the cup from her hands. "You never know where magic is going to come from. All you have to do is give it a chance."

"I just feel funny having a good time when I'm not supposed to."

"Who says you're not supposed to? Baby, you have been sad long enough. We all have been. And we will be again, don't you worry. You have yourself some fun whenever you can. Never give up a chance to smile."

But suddenly it wasn't Beanie talking, and Noelle wasn't on the snowy ground at Potomac Middle School. She was back in the shoe department at Simon's, warm as toast, wearing shiny yellow Hunter boots.

Chapter 4

"How did you do that?"

"How did I do what?" Charlie asked, guileless.

"That whole story. All the things that would have happened if I had gone out that night instead of staying at home."

"I didn't do anything, you did."

"I was telling you a memory and suddenly it went into a whole different thing!"

"We have choices all the time, and different outcomes for each choice, you know."

I felt irritated. Charlie seemed to be being deliberately obtuse, when we both knew she . . . well, what? What *did* we both know about her?

"I *know*, but we don't always see the outcome," I said, well aware that I was beginning to believe the unbelievable. "Was that really what you think would have happened if I'd gone to my aunt's that Christmas Eve after my mother died?"

"Do I think *what* would have happened?"

I narrowed my eyes at Charlie. "Come on."

"That bit you told at the end? About sleigh riding? I assume so, yes. You would have had a grand time."

"Would have had," I echoed to myself. As it was, I'd had a miserable night, exactly as anyone could have predicted for a kid who opted to throw herself into a pillow and cry about the loss of her mother. It was totally miserable, completely heartbreaking.

And I didn't really blame myself for that, truth be told, because it was a really hard time. It was a very hard thing to ask a kid in my position to rally and go out to have fun. Apparently it was possible, but for some reason grief has a stronger pull than anything else. Both laughter and tears were a release, and, boy, I needed a release. I guess the fact is that the tears were a more sure release. When I thought about it now, the big fear really was that I'd have gone to

my aunt's and gone out with my cousins and tried to have
fun in a crowd but would have been thinking instead about
all my sadness, and having to hold it in all night. That
would have been miserable.

I wasn't wrong to have been cautious.

I only wish I'd known how much better it would have
gone if I'd taken that chance.

"Still," I found myself saying, "that's one instance of
erring on the side of caution. I don't think I can blame
myself for it."

"Child, there is *always* a better option than sitting
around feeling sorry for yourself."

I thought of the many times I'd gone out because "it
would be good for me" and ended up feeling alone and
lonely in a crowd. "I don't think that's true," I said.

"Tell me another story, then," Charlie said, and stood
up to rifle though the shoes, her broad bottom knocking
against the wall and the shelf alternately.

I kept organizing. "I don't have any great stories."

"You could! And anyway, I'll be the judge of that!"

I picked up some chunky sneakers, a thick-soled, bright-
colored remnant from my past. "Good lord, these are

Etnies! I didn't even know they still made these!" I turned them over and looked at the price, then gave a low whistle. "Wish I'd kept my old ones."

"You wore those boots?" Charlie asked.

I laughed. "They're not boots. They're sneakers. Kind of. Anyway, yes, there was this fashion craze where girls all wanted to look like they were wearing their boyfriends' clothes, and these"—I held up the shoes—"these were perfect for it."

"Indeed." She looked like she found the idea distasteful.

"For what it's worth," I said with a shrug, "I don't have very romantic memories of them myself. But you want another story? I know another one."

*

No one had ever dreaded New Year's Eve more.

Noelle had made tentative plans—okay, no, they were *plans*—to join her friend Maura's family on a dinner cruise on the Potomac River. When they started talking about it in September, it seemed perfectly fine, even fun. Certainly a uniquely D.C. thing to do.

But as time wore on and Noelle's fear of terrorism grew with the news stories, so did her fear of being vulnerable, on a boat, on a river, in D.C. on New Year's Eve. This was a big one, too. The concern over possible attacks on millennium celebrations had put everyone on high alert. But no one seemed on higher alert than Noelle.

So it was an awkward moment when Maura called that afternoon to solidify their plans.

"I can't go," Noelle said, then manufactured a cough. "I—I'm not feeling well."

"What? You were fine yesterday!"

"It came on suddenly."

"Noelle! My parents bought you a ticket and everything!"

She coughed again, but it did nothing to hide her shame. So she overcompensated, making her voice weaker. "I'm really sorry. Try Tiffany. I bet she'd take my ticket in a heartbeat."

"Right. Tell me what sixteen-year-old has no plans for New Year's Eve at the last minute. I can't believe you're doing this to me. Do you know how much that ticket cost?"

No, do you? Noelle wanted to ask, but that would have

been unnecessarily snarky. The ticket probably *did* cost a lot, and she *was* a jerk for canceling at the last minute, but she knew she'd be no fun for anyone if she made herself go, because she was so scared there was going to be a terrorist attack if she went.

And only if she went. In some weird twist of logic, she felt certain that she was the variable that would make it happen. She wasn't at all worried for her friends who would go without her, because she knew they'd be safe. It was *she* who would bring the bad luck.

Someone had told her that was called "magical thinking."

All she knew was that it sucked, and part of her tried really really hard to talk herself into going, but she couldn't find the courage.

"Are you sure you won't come?" Maura pleaded.

Guilt tightened inside Noelle, but she remained resolute. "I'm really sorry."

The moment she and Maura hung up—Maura slamming her phone down—she felt better.

Relieved.

She didn't exactly feel like she'd saved the world—her

worry about disaster didn't extend to giving herself credit for heroism if she didn't create it—but she did, at least, feel like she could have a peaceful night at home.

So she called her boyfriend, Mark Delgado, and told him she was going to be home for the evening and he could come join her.

He sounded less excited than she'd hoped. "I have plans, Nolly. I'm going to Stu Freedman's party."

She waited a moment for him to invite her along, even though she didn't want to go, but no invitation was forthcoming, so she managed to feel even more disenfranchised than before.

"Are you serious?" she asked. "You don't want to come spend New Year's Eve with me?"

"I saw you two nights ago!"

"I know, but it's *New Year's!*" How could he not see the significance? It was almost like saying he was going to his buddy's to play pool and beer pong on Valentine's Day, but she should be fine because they already saw each other that week.

"I guess I could come by if you really want me to," he said with such reluctance she could see him as a cartoon character literally dragging his feet and digging trenches in the dirt behind him.

"Yes, I really want you to."

"Fine." It was hard for her to pretend that was a rousing, enthusiastic response, but she had to pretend she didn't notice it was the exact opposite. "Great! I'll see you soon!"

They hung up, and she ran upstairs to put her makeup on, throw curlers in her hair, and put on her oh-so-casual sk8er boi look, with torn jeans, a big T-shirt, and Etnies on her feet. She didn't want to look like she was trying too hard, but, man, she was trying so hard.

Mark showed up, looking sullen. "Hey."

"Hi!" She ushered him into the kitchen. She hadn't had time to make anything yet, but at least she knew what was there and had plans. "I've got chips and dip, and a bunch of cheeses, and Cap'n Crunch if you're in a seafaring mood—"

"I'm fine, thanks."

"Oh. Okay. Well, want something to drink? Coke? I think my dad has some beer in the fridge."

"Nah, I'm not staying too long, and I don't want to

drink and drive." He raked a hand through his too-long sandy blond hair. He looked like Shaggy from *Scooby-Doo*, only without the flesh-colored goatee that would have pushed him over the edge into Nowhereland as far as her attraction to him went.

The gesture, though—that got to her. Something in her deflated. "What do you mean you're not staying long? It's only nine thirty. It's two and a half hours till midnight."

"Right . . ."

"You're staying for that, right?" She already knew the answer. He wasn't.

His face took on a pained expression, though she didn't think it was sincere, and he said, "About that. I told Stu I'd go to his party, and he's really bummed at the idea that I might not make it, so I'm sorry, I just really gotta head on over there."

Once again she waited for the invitation to join him—which she was more determined than ever not to accept—and once again the invitation did not come.

"You know what?" she said. "Why don't you just go?" Her voice was tight with anger.

He, on the other hand, looked relieved. "Really? You mean it?"

"Oh yeah, I mean it. Go."

"Aw, man, you're the best." He moved in to kiss her cheek—*seriously, my cheek?*—but she pushed him away.

"Go and don't come back, how's that? Ever."

"Wait," he said stupidly. "What? Don't ever come back?"

She shook her head. "Never."

"So . . . you're breaking up with me?"

"Yup. Happy New Year, Mark. I really enjoyed this time we had together." She was on the verge of tears now. Not because Mark mattered so much. They'd only been dating for about four months, and he was pretty much a bore. Plus he hadn't gotten her anything for Christmas. Which, okay, maybe he didn't have any money, but he could have *made* something. Any little symbolic thing would have done.

If it's the thought that counts and there is no thought, well, that counts.

"You're serious."

"As a heart attack."

"All because I want to go to Stu's."

"No, all because you're a selfish jerk." It was on the tip of her tongue to mention the lack of a Christmas gift (she'd given him a nice wallet for him to put his nothing in), and the fact that he hadn't had the consideration to include her tonight, but all of that sounded like sour grapes, and she knew it. She wasn't going to give him the satisfaction of sounding like a bitter shrew he was better off without.

"Fine, *fine*, you win."

"I win?"

"I'll call Stu and tell him I'll be late."

Late. Not *not going*, just late.

"Tell him when you get there," she said, knowing it didn't make sense but not caring. "Because I don't want you here."

"You're crazy."

"No, I'm not! You're just so selfish you'll never have any clue what I'm feeling." She picked up the coat he'd taken off when he walked in and shoved it into his hands, pushing him toward the door at the same time. "Just *go*."

"Okay, okay, I'm going. But you'll regret this."

"I doubt it."

He went out the front door, the storm door slamming behind him. She watched his dark figure retreat into the darkness.

She could not believe this. Could. Not. Believe it. How did every single holiday always seem to suck? Really and truly, it was getting comical. She hadn't been expecting anything great tonight, but she'd still been going into it cheerfully. Really, it would have been perfectly fine sitting on the couch with Mark, eating Doritos and watching TV. It was hardly a dreamy romantic New Year's Eve, but it would have done.

She wasn't a demanding person, she really wasn't.

But this was what she'd ended up with. Herself. Maybe it was better, but it didn't feel so great at the moment.

She slumped upstairs to change her clothes and maybe find some magazines to occupy her while she watched the New Year's shows and felt her youth slip by.

Minutes later, she heard a racket at the door and ran down, expecting Mark to be back, head held low in shame for having abandoned her, but it was her father with a woman she'd never met before.

His surprised expression must have mirrored hers.

"Noelle!"

"Dad? What are you doing here?"

"I'm . . . we're . . ." He pointed to the woman and himself, then said, "I don't think you've met Carla?"

"No." He knew darn well she hadn't met *Carla*. In fact, if he had been dating—and he must have been—she hadn't met any of his dates since her mother had died four years ago. So *Carla* must be something special if he'd deemed her worthy to bring home.

She looked special, in that way that men liked. Tall, incredibly thin, with really impossibly large breasts. Her glossy dark hair shone in the hall light, the chin-length bob swinging with every small movement she made.

"Hi, Noelle," Carla said. She had a light accent, probably southern, and drew out the name, *Noeelllle*. "I've heard so much about you. I've been dying to meet you."

"Have you?" Noelle hated herself for not having a better game face. She wanted to look friendly, or at least not hostile, but her expression felt sarcastic. She felt like a homely hulk compared to this woman. She turned to her father. "I hadn't heard."

He looked rattled. "I've been meaning to introduce you for a while now, but the time never seemed right."

"Mm-hm."

"So," he went on, "what are *you* doing here? I thought you were going down to D.C."

"I changed my mind. Mark was here for a while, and he had something else to do. He might come back, I don't know." But she did know. She knew there was no way he was coming back, even if he were being chased by rhinos.

"Oh! Oh, okay. That's fine, then. I just needed to pick something up, and we'll be going back out."

Carla looked puzzled, and he shot her a look that she didn't seem to understand but that Noelle knew meant *shhh, I'll explain it all to you later.*

"Are you off to Stu Freedman's party, too?" Noelle muttered bitterly.

"Beg your pardon?" Carla asked. Her father just looked uncomfortable.

"Nothing. Just a joke. A lame joke."

Her father went upstairs—presumably to get the manufactured something he needed, leaving Noelle and Carla to stand in uncomfortable silence for a couple minutes—then, coming back down, he said, "I got it. Carla, are you ready?"

Carla still looked confused but, to her credit, at least she knew better than to blow his whole act by straight-up saying she had no idea what was going on. "I guess I am," she said. "Yes." Then she turned to Noelle and took her hand in hers and said, with very kind sincerity, "It was so nice to meet you, honey. I hope I'll see you again real soon."

"Thanks," Noelle said, because she couldn't think of anything else.

And they were off. He didn't tell her he wouldn't be home—that would have been way too awkward for everyone—but she knew it. So she went upstairs, put on her flannel pajamas, washed her makeup off, and came back down to sit on the couch with a big bowl of Cap'n Crunch to watch Dick Clark ring in the new year.

Chapter 5

A re you sure you won't come?" Maura pleaded.

They were off and running on another rewriting of history. Noelle was aware of it—she was looking right at the cloppy shoes that seemed to be magically taking her through time—but she was utterly powerless against it. She had to go along for the ride.

"Are you sure you won't come?"

Guilt tightened inside Noelle. She couldn't do this to her friend. She couldn't do it to Maura's parents, who had bought the extra ticket so that her daughter could take a friend along. She knew it was stupid and selfish to suggest that Maura take someone else at the last minute; she was only trying to get herself off the hook.

Well, she'd said she'd go, and she was going to do it.

Even though she really, *really* didn't want to.

"I'm sorry, Maura," she said. Then, because it sounded like she was refusing, she quickly added, "Of course I'll go. It's just a little headache. I'll take some Tylenol, and I'm sure I'll be fine later."

"Oh, thank God!" Maura sounded genuinely relieved. "My parents would have killed me if I'd wasted that ticket!"

For a moment, Noelle envied her the parents who might get mad. The parents who had made plans and allowed her to invite a friend along. The parents who were parents—plural—and neither of them had ever died or left. The feeling she had wasn't just laziness about going, or a homebody's impulse to stay in and mope; it was jealousy.

It was mostly fear, but there was an element of jealousy. Like, if there was an emergency, that family would group together, but who would be there for her?

Silly, she knew, but that's how she thought.

That night, as the small dinner-cruise ship *Esworthy* glided out of the dock, Noelle was very glad she was on board. This was no huge *Titanic* ship, rocking on the ocean (of course). It was just like an average-size restaurant with a lobby, dinner tables, elaborate restrooms, and a pretty large band on a very small stage.

They were playing "Jingle Bells" as Noelle and company walked into the room, and she was immediately in a more festive mood. It was hard to argue with the fun of dashing through the snow, and all but impossible to ignore the forced cheer of the décor.

The walls were a dark cream color with lots of gold touches—gilded trim, gilded paisley tapestries held back with golden ropes and tassels. Holly circled every sconce, flickering candles glittered on all the tables, and mistletoe hung strategically here and there, in places where people were likely to stop and talk.

In the air there was a scent of fresh pine, so deliciously strong that it had to be piped in artificially. But a surprisingly balmy breeze blew in every time someone opened the door to come in from outside, and the scent of the river, along with the pine, was a heady combination.

The view outside was even more beautiful than the one

inside, if possible, and Maura and Noelle wrapped themselves in their coats and went out and sat on the bow of the boat, looking at the monuments—lit like toys in a tiny train set—as they slid past them through the dark night.

There were a surprising number of boats on the Potomac around them, and something about that was reassuring. All the little vessels were variously lit up, and most of them were festooned with string lights—some red and green, some blue and white, a few so etched in white lights that they looked like they were covered in brilliant diamonds, reflecting in the gently moving water.

"I know you would rather have been with Mark tonight," Maura said. "If I had a boyfriend, I probably would have wanted to stay home and be with him, too."

Noelle fixed her eyes on the wide, low, brightly lit Kennedy Center in the distance, its clone shadow dancing on the river. "No," she said. The water slapped against the hull of the boat. "I really don't wish I were with him. He always lets me down. Tonight probably wouldn't have been any exception."

"Then why didn't you want to come?"

Noelle's pride wanted her to insist on her headache story, but Maura knew it wasn't true, and Noelle had more respect for her than to continue the lie, even though the truth was so embarrassing. "I was scared."

"Scared of *what?*"

The peace out here was incredible. It made her truth sound even stupider. "Terrorists."

"Oh." Maura nodded. No questions. No mocking. "You're probably not the only one. Actually, I can't say it didn't occur to me."

"Really?"

"Obviously. It's, like, all we hear about on the news anymore." She pointed to the Washington Monument. "And we're in about the most iconic American place possible." She smiled. "But I feel a hundred percent safe, don't you?"

"I do." Noelle smiled. She really did. This was stunningly beautiful. She'd never forget it. What a way to ring in the new year.

"How come you stay with him?" Maura asked.

"What?"

"Mark," she said. "If he always lets you down, how come you're with him?"

Noelle gave a short laugh. "The answer to that is even more humiliating."

"Come on."

She shrugged and thought about how to word it. "I think I stay with him because I don't want to be alone."

"Hey, I like being with you, you should, too." Maura laughed. "But, seriously, I kind of get what you mean. It's not quite a status thing to have a boyfriend, but it sure feels like a status thing *not* to."

"That's it exactly," Noelle said, feeling like Maura had just come up with one of the most profound points she'd ever heard. *"Exactly."*

"Ironic, huh?"

"Totally. And it's weird, because I used to totally love being alone. I loved faking sick and staying home and being alone while my dad was at work." She felt a wave of shame as she realized she'd been trying to do the same to Maura. "And I used to love having Saturday nights to watch terrible TV, eat junk food, and have sleepovers. Then somewhere along the way everything changed and I got weird about it."

"Like you feel like a total loser if you're home alone on Friday or Saturday night? Even if no one else knows?"

"Yes."

"Or on New Year's Eve?"

They both laughed.

"Or *Valentine's* Day," Noelle added. "Man, Valentine's Day is the absolute worst, isn't it?"

"I'll say."

Noelle felt warmth spread through her. "We girls should just stick together better. Make our own plans and stop feeling like we need guys so much. To hell with anyone who thinks we need guys. We don't."

Maura held out her hand. "Deal."

Noelle shook it. "Deal."

"Except we kind of do."

"I know." They both laughed again.

"Now, let's get back inside," Maura said. "It's almost midnight, and there were some cute guys in there." She gave a trill of laughter.

"Maura!"

"I know, I know, but I could swear I saw Jake Marsden."

The name rang a bell, but Noelle couldn't quite place him. "Who?" she asked.

Maura stopped to look at her as if she were the biggest moron on the ship. "Football player? I don't know what he plays, but he looks good in his uniform. Dark hair, blue eyes? *Gorgeous* smile?"

"You're not really ringing any bells for me."

"He just transferred back to Churchill from Gonzaga."

"Ooooh, the transfer guy." She had seen him, but only from a distance. They said he'd gone to their middle school for a while, too, before transferring to Gonzaga, a private Catholic high school in D.C., but she didn't really remember him from there either.

Still, something about the name, or maybe the idea of him, rang a very distant bell with her.

The boat banked to the left and began to turn around. Inside, people started counting backward from twenty toward midnight.

"We have to hurry!" Maura took off like Cinderella, down the steps and into the main dining hall.

"I'm coming," Noelle called behind her, but she took

her time. She didn't need to be in the middle of the chaos and clapping and kissing and shaking hands with strangers. It was more fun to keep her back to the quiet outside and feel the cool wind on her cheeks and in her hair.

As soon as the band began to play "Auld Lang Syne," she went in. The pressure was over, and the boat was returning to its dock. Now the band would play a few more songs and people would dance.

Maybe she'd see about this Jake Marsden guy.

And she did, almost right away. Once she knew to look for him, it was obvious—the tall, good-looking kid, about seventeen, standing next to an older woman. Maybe his grandmother? How sweet of him, looking after the old lady. There was also a couple with them, his parents, obviously. That seemed to be about it.

"Let's go over there," Maura said.

"We can't! It will be so obvious!"

"I don't care. It's easier than trying to get near him at school—Kathy Coats is always hanging around him."

Noelle hung back. "Is that his girlfriend?"

Maura snorted. "She wishes. But no, she's not."

They were making their way through the crowd. The pine scent was now obscured by perfumes, colognes, lingering tobacco smoke, and alcohol breath. More than one older man leaned down a little too leeringly as Noelle excused herself trying to get past.

Finally they made it to the other side of the room and near where Jake Marsden still stood with his group.

"Now what?" Maura asked through her teeth.

"*I* don't know, *you're* the one who led us over here!"

"Yeah, well, now I'm the one who wants to run back because this was a stupid idea. We are *so obvious.*"

Embarrassment crept up Noelle's spine and multiplied when she met Jake's eyes. He smiled and gave a little wave. Did he recognize her? Why would he? But she recognized him, now that she was near him. So she had to play it cool.

She gave a little wave back.

"What are you *doing?*" Maura asked in a stage whisper.

"He *waved,*" Noelle returned in the same.

"Oh my God, what are we going to do?"

"Excuse me." Suddenly he was there. Right there with

them. Looking right down into Noelle's face. "Don't you go to Churchill?"

"Yes," she said, then, with a cool she didn't know she possessed, put her hand out. "Noelle Carpenter."

"Jacob Marsden," he said, taking her hand and shaking it awkwardly. Was it possible that *he* was the nervous one? "I've seen you around."

"I think I might have seen you, too," she said.

The music shifted from "Sunrise, Sunset" to something jazzier. She thought it was a Glenn Miller tune, a little peppier than the last one, but still a slow dance.

Which mattered because Jake asked, "Not to be weird or anything, but do you want to dance?"

She smiled at him, even though her heart was pounding ridiculously and she felt the warmth rising in her cheeks. "Are we old enough?" she asked, indicating the general demographic of the place.

"Probably not," he said. "Let's do it anyway."

Noelle felt Maura push her from behind. "Go!" came in a very small hiss behind her.

"Okay," she said, more to Maura than to Jake, but the

moment he took her in his arms, she wasn't thinking of anyone in the entire world besides him.

She'd never danced in this formal grown-up style before, but he led her so easily, she felt like a professional.

"This is wonderful," she said breathlessly, unable to keep her enthusiasm inside. It was like a dream. Like the dance scene in *Beauty and the Beast* or *Anastasia*.

"Where have you been all night? What kind of Cinderella only shows up after midnight?"

She laughed. "I always seem to get everything backwards."

"Does that mean you're going to ask me on a date?"

"I beg your pardon?" But she'd heard him. Hadn't she? She'd heard him perfectly.

"If you do things backwards, are you going to ask me on a date? Or are you more traditional than that?"

"I'm *way* more traditional than that." Where her boldness was coming from, she didn't know. But something about him made it easy. She felt like she knew him already, even though she didn't know him at all.

"In that case," he said, "I'll ask you. What was your name again?"

"Noelle."

"Oh, Noelle. Of course. I knew the face, but . . . Okay, Noelle. Will you go out with me on Friday night?"

All thoughts of Mark flew out the door. "Yes," she said. "Yes, I will."

Chapter 6

That didn't happen," I said to Charlie, taking off the Etnies. "How did you conjure all of that up?"

"I told you, dear, I'm your guardian angel. It's my *job* to come here and remind you that you have many choices in your life, and, unfortunately, well . . . you keep making the choices that keep you from living the life you're supposed to live."

"I *am* living the life I'm supposed to live!"

"If you say so, dear."

"I am!"

"Very good."

"Well, what's *your* life like, then? I can't help but notice you're here on Christmas Eve, same as me, and you didn't want to call anyone and tell them where you were, so you must not have had the most wonderful plans tonight yourself."

"I think tonight's plans are very rewarding indeed," Charlie objected. "Not easy, heaven knows, but certainly *rewarding.*"

"Those plans being . . . ?"

"Reforming you. So to speak. Best I can, anyway. I don't mean to sound cross, but you are one tough nut to crack." Charlie's round, red face burst into a smile. Her blue eyes shone, and, honestly, if it weren't for the dress, she could almost have passed for Santa Claus.

That would have been a heck of a twist on a Christmas story. Santa as a sort of crazy old lady character, being both a little bit St. Nick and a lot Mrs. Claus, aka Charlie.

There was a certain symmetry to it.

"What are you smiling at, Nolly?"

"Oh, nothing, I was just thinking of—wait, what did you call me?"

"Nolly. Isn't that right?"

My stomach lurched. "How did you know that?"

"It was in the notes, dear. It *is* your nickname, isn't it? We're supposed to use nicknames whenever comfortably possible so that the subject eases into trusting us."

"Subject? Trust? What, did you go to some sort of cult school?"

"Of course not. It's from"—she jabbed her finger upward as she had before—"above."

I sighed and pulled the Etnies off my feet. "Well, if you're trying to gain my trust, you're on the wrong track. You're freaking me out. No one has called me Nolly in years."

"Ah, then, you see? How *else* could I have known it without some divine intervention?"

It was a good question. I studied her closely to try to remember if I recognized the face as that of some sort of old friend of the family or something. Someone who would have had an *in* to private information like that.

Although why anyone would be *interested* in having an in like that and using it, I couldn't really imagine. I wasn't that interesting. In fact, as Charlie herself was pointing out, I was a woman who rarely took chances, who almost never went anywhere, and who didn't even have all that many people in her close circle.

I'd be one of the worst targets for any sort of scam.

I put the Etnies into their box and put it on the shelf. "This is just weird," I said. "Plain old weird." I found a gray Prada pump and looked for its mate.

Charlie handed it to me, as if by magic. I had neither seen the shoe nor seen Charlie sneak up on me. I put the pair in their box and put it back on the shelf.

"What about this, dear: What if you simply *try* to believe for just a moment? I think it would make all of this so much easier."

Intellectually it sounded like more predator talk, but I didn't feel an ounce of fear. I just felt this was a crazy old lady looking for some purpose on a lonely Christmas Eve.

She probably hadn't gotten trapped in here on purpose. That would have been a very hard thing to predict and plan on. Even I hadn't realized that Lex would close the store early.

Maybe she was just a sad old lady who had come in

from the cold and found herself locked in and in need of a purpose so she didn't just look . . . foolish.

But how *did* she know so much about me?

How did she manage to manipulate my imagination so that, for every memory I had, I was able to see an alternate outcome?

"Everything you can even imagine happening in your life could have happened if you'd gone a different direction," Charlie answered, as if I had asked the question aloud.

But I knew I hadn't.

"I beg your pardon?"

"You were wondering what I was doing to put stories in your head, weren't you?"

"No." Lie.

"Well, it would be natural if you were," Charlie said, unbothered by my denial. "And the answer, *if* you were wondering that, would be that our lives are like . . . what do you call it? A highway. A big long road with lots of turns off of it. You can take any of those roads to get to the end. You can even turn around on them and come back to a road you were on before. That's what the timid tend to do."

I didn't say it, but I had the sense that I fell into that category. *The timid.* Had I returned to an old "safe" road in my own life? I felt I had, probably many times. An astrologer once told me I was a typical Cancer: "the crab who creeps out of its home, looks around and gets scared to death, then runs back in."

Well, that was about the size of it.

The speakers kept on playing holiday music, as they did 'round the clock, and in the distance I could hear the sound of Elvis singing "Blue Christmas." It reminded me of a snowstorm when I was in college, but I dared not mention it to Charlie for fear that I'd be transported yet again to another regret.

And that, I thought suddenly, seemed like a good point. "If you are here to show me the error of my ways, so to speak, what good do you imagine it does to make me regret my choices?"

"Why, child!" Charlie looked genuinely surprised. "Are you not heartened by the idea that those sad times could have been turned into happy times?"

"They weren't, though, so it's not really so heartening."

"But you're so young still—"

I snorted. I didn't feel young. In fact, some days I felt downright old. *Ancient.*

"—and you still have so many choices to make. Don't you think it's *helpful* to see how very *well* things can go when you try something out of your comfort zone?"

"I've been out of my comfort zone many times and lived to regret it," I retorted. "Trust me."

"Let's look around the store," Charlie said suddenly.

"What?" I indicated the still-large pile of shoes strewn across the floor. "We've got our work cut out for us here."

"Oh, come on, dear, we're in such a unique situation. Let's have fun with it. Let's go to the *toy* department!"

I barely heard her. I just kept collecting one shoe, looking for the second, then finding the box and shelving them. I was like an automated robot, doing one single job. "Let's finish here before we go out wandering anywhere."

"You don't even know how much snow is out there!"

"Apparently it's enough to keep us trapped in here."

"But don't you want to see it? What is more beautiful than a freshly fallen blanket of snow?"

"It'll be there when we finish." I wasn't going to insist

that Charlie help, because, frankly, she wasn't that good at it. Yes, the mess might be her fault, but the poor thing seemed to have done it by accident. And if she was speaking with sincerity, then even though I knew this wasn't really my guardian angel, maybe the woman thought she was; maybe she thought she was really destined to help people, in which case I should probably just shut up and not tell her to pipe down and let me work at fixing her mistake.

So, fun as it did sound, I still couldn't just stop working and dillydally around the store when there was this chaos to straighten out.

"Cup of tea in Filigree?" Charlie suggested.

"No, thank you."

There was a moment of silence, and then Charlie said, "You know, I guess I'm just going to go pick out a bed to sleep in tonight. We *are* stuck for the night, are we not?"

"We do seem to be."

"Well, my goodness, I have already found this exhausting, so I'd just as soon go pick out my sleeping place."

"All right, all right." I didn't want her wandering

around the store by herself. "I'll take you to the bedding department and maybe you can catch some shut-eye now, eh?"

Charlie shook her head. "Certainly not. I have my work to do."

"Your work?"

"You might as well start believing me. It will save ever so much time and energy for us both."

The truth was, part of me did believe her. Or at least wanted to. But her story was so preposterous that I couldn't truly go with it. Guardian angel. Not unless I was asleep and this was all a dream. But I'd had realistic dreams before, and none went on as long as this.

And if dreams were the work of the subconscious, I honestly wasn't sure I was this creative.

No, this—whatever it was—this was real.

"I have an idea!" Charlie said. "I have the most *wonderful* idea!"

"What's that?"

"Do you play checkers?"

The question was so unexpected that I laughed. "Not

in years, no. But yes. I mean yes, sort of." I shook my head, tangled in my own surprise. "Why?"

"How would you like to make a little wager?"

"What's that?"

Charlie's face fell a little. "It's a bet. I predict one thing and you predict another and one of us wins and—"

"I know what a wager is," I said, a bit impatient. "I meant what wager did you have in mind?"

"We play a game of checkers. If I win, you tell another story from your past."

I considered this with amusement. "And if I win?"

"Then *you* tell another story from your past."

"Tricky. I see what you did there."

Charlie beamed, and her whole pudgy face lit up. "Do we have a deal?"

"Sure." Why not? It was eleven thirty on Christmas Eve and we had the entire night to pass before—surely!— the salt trucks and plows would come through and clear out the streets so we could leave.

"Let's do it!" Charlie said, then danced her way toward the toy department, lighter on her feet than I would have imagined she could be. "Let's go!"

The toy department was fully lit and as delightful as one could imagine. It was something else Simon's was famous for—even in a world where online sales had taken over the retail market for mass-marketed toys, Simon's managed to stay relevant with a wonderful collection of specialty toys that were heirloom quality yet, at the same time, genuinely engaging and fun.

"Here's a board," she said. A checker- or chessboard wasn't hard to find in Simon's toy department, but she did pick the most beautiful, a hand-painted one made from carved white oak.

We sat down on either side of a table and played, agreeing on two out of three for the win.

If there was such a thing as a checkers savant, it had to be said Charlie could fit the bill. There was not a move I could make that Charlie couldn't counter. It was almost as if she had God whispering in her ear on how to win. Which, of course, she would have said she did, but she didn't. Not really.

Charlie beat me handily two games in a row.

"Fine," I said, trying to repress my laughter. She was going to get her way. *Of course* she was! "One more. But we're going to work on the shoes while I tell it."

"Certainly we are. You're going to have to find an appropriate pair to wear."

"Oh, is that part of the rules?"

"It has been so far, hasn't it?"

I smiled. "Well, why on earth not? To the shoe department!"

Chapter 7

We went back and spent about an hour sorting through the shoes and putting them away. It was surprising how much we got done, and it was a good thing, too, because it needed to be tidy in there.

But when I came across a gorgeous pair of Manolo Blahniks—yes, yes, I know, old school, not the newest thing on the market—I couldn't resist putting them on.

Prior to that, I hadn't been able to come up with a good story, but, I swear, the moment I slipped them on, it was like magic. Like enchantment. Like, it was hard to admit, the work of a guardian angel.

The words just came to me.

＊

In her midtwenties, about five years ago, Noelle found herself at a holiday party given by someone whose name she never could remember when she thought about it later. In fact, as she pictured the scene, she didn't even recognize a great many of the faces, so she thought it might have been a friend of a friend of a friend.

All she really remembered was that her friend Suz was there, and the reason she remembered that was because Suz was drunk to beat the band and sobbing about some ex-boyfriend of hers, whose name she also didn't remember. Eric? Maybe it was Eric. Whoever he was, he wasn't memorable enough to stick with her.

But, boy, had he stuck with Suz that night.

"I'm . . . never . . . going"—sob—"to . . . find . . . someone . . . like him." Hiccup. Sob. I'm pretty sure she swiped snot out from under her nose with her forearm. "I . . . *can't* . . ."

It was embarrassing. She was a total mess.

"Listen, Suz, let's go. I think you need to sleep this off."

"Go? *Go?* I can't go. I can't *go*. He might come."

"In that case, you *definitely* should get out of here."

"No." She shook her head. Resolute. "I have to wait. If he comes, then I can *explain* everything to him."

Noelle had noticed, in her lifetime, that if there's one thing people don't want after a breakup, it is for the other part of the breakup to *explain everything.* She always thought that about the poor guy in that Adele song— maybe he didn't *want* to clear the evening to *go over everything.*

She was pretty sure Eric or whatever his name was wasn't going to want to do that tonight. Hell, it was two days before Christmas. Everyone was supposed to be festive and happy. This was a catastrophe.

"Listen," she said to Suz. "You stay sitting right here. Okay? Stay right here, and I'm going to go get you some coffee."

"And a pinot grigio," she said with a nod.

"No. *No more wine.* Coffee. If he comes, you need to have your wits about you, right? So you can talk to him?" Man, she hoped the poor guy somehow had the sense to not show up. "So you just wait right here, and I'm going to get that coffee."

"Okay," she said, and her head slumped down. She might have been asleep before Noelle even turned to head for the kitchen.

And a good thing, too. There was nothing Suz needed more than sleep. Except maybe to get out of there and prevent the almost-certain embarrassment and humiliation that she was going to bring down upon herself if she stayed.

There was a DJ at the party, playing a fun mix of modern holiday music, some of which she'd never heard before. At a table in the corner, a psychic was doing five-minute readings for whoever wanted them. Elsewhere a massage therapist had set up a chair for doing shoulder and neck massages for guests.

She'd never remember who the host or hostess was, but whoever it was, they'd certainly done it right.

She went into the kitchen and found an electric kettle. She heated it up, determined to make coffee from ground beans and a paper towel filter if need be, but fortunately she found a jar of General Foods International coffee in Café Vienna flavor over the stove.

"That's no fun," a voice said behind her shoulder.

She turned to see a strikingly hot guy with dark hair and light eyes, his mouth quirked into a half-smile. "Coffee?"

"No thanks." He raised a glass of something amber and serious-looking to her. "I'm set."

"No, I meant, the coffee? What's no fun?"

"Oh, yes. The coffee. The drink of the nearly departed. Are you leaving?"

Noelle frowned, scrutinizing his vaguely familiar face. "Do we know each other?"

"We do not."

She had no time for this. "Okay, well, it was nice almost meeting you." The water was boiling, and she found a mug to stir the powder and water into.

He hesitated, and she sensed he wasn't nearly as confident as his manner had suggested, but he didn't say anything else. Instead he slipped away, back into the next room.

She followed shortly after, holding the mug and looking like the world's least fun partygoer, but as long as she could get the caffeine into Suz, she didn't care.

"You there!" Noelle looked around. It was the fortune-teller, pointing at her. "Yes, you. Come this way."

"I . . . can't." She nodded at the coffee and gave an apologetic smile. "Sorry."

"But I have a sign from the other side for you. Do you not want to know about your love life? There is a tall, dark, and handsome man very close to you, closer than you think . . ."

She laughed out loud. "If tonight is any advertisement for love, no thank you. Sorry." She didn't want to be rude. "I just have to get this to my friend." As she walked away, back to Suz, she could have sworn she heard the gypsy woman say, "Sorry, Jake. I tried."

She went back to Suz and basically poured the hot liquid down her throat. "Can you get up and get to the car?" she asked her.

"You don't need to go," Suz said, then hiccupped. "I'll go, but you can stay. I know I need to go. He's . . . not . . ." She dissolved into tears again. "You stay. I can take a cab."

"No way," Noelle said. "I'm going to take you back. There is no way I'm pouring you into a cab at this point."

"It's fine." But it sounded like she said *sfine*. "I mean it. I don't want to ruin your night."

Suz was definitely not fine.

"Come on." She gave her the last sip of the Café Vienna, then hoisted her up.

"Do you need help?" It was the guy with the dark hair and light eyes, hurrying over. No one else even seemed to notice them.

"Oh hiiiiiiii," Suz said upon seeing him.

Lord, it was easy to see where this could go. From bad to worse, real damn quick.

"No thanks," Noelle said. "We're just leaving. But thank you. Seriously."

"Are you sure?" He looked concerned. But by then Suz was walking on her own, if unsteadily, and there was no need for a knight in shining armor to push his way in.

"Thank you," Noelle said again, and walked Suz carefully out into the cold and to the car.

✝

There was no point in elaborating on the story for Charlie. It was just more of the same. More party, more stranger, more embarrassment, more drunken mess. Then a silent drive back with a passed-out Suz, and that was about it.

To elaborate would just be to whine. It was another crummy holiday, it was that simple.

"But those shoes," Charlie said, pointing to the Manolo Blahniks. "Something about those shoes inspired you to tell it."

Shrug. "Nothing that interesting. I got some shoes like this for the party that night, for the whole holiday season actually, and that's all that reminded me. Don't women always buy shoes and clothes with a scene in mind? My scene had nothing to do with the reality I ended up with, believe me."

"Such a pity."

"You have some magic you can do to make me see why I should have left my drunk friend passed out on the couch?"

"Certainly not!" Charlie gave a mysterious smile. "But I do think there are better alternatives."

*

"You don't need to go," Suz said, then hiccupped. "I'll go, but you can stay. I know I need to go. He's . . . not . . ." She dissolved into tears again. "You stay. I can take a cab."

"No way," Noelle said. "I'm going to take you back. There is no way I'm pouring you into a cab at this point."

"It's fine."

Noelle hesitated. *Was* it fine? Suz didn't seem on the verge of throwing up or passing out anymore. "Let me get you a coffee and see how you feel," she said, considering staying, not because the party was that great but simply because it was *always* her impulse to leave, and she *always* followed her impulses, and thus she never stuck around to see if anything different might ever happen in her life.

"Make it a double," Suz said as Noelle got up.

"You got it."

She went into the kitchen and found some instant coffee, had a couple of words with an unusually good-looking guy, then took the drink back to Suz, who seemed a little more with it than she had when Noelle had left.

"He's a jerk," Suz said.

"Who is?" Noelle asked, still thinking of the good-looking guy she'd seen in the kitchen.

"Eric," Suz answered, as if it were obvious. Actually, it probably was. That's who she'd been talking about all night long.

"Yes, he is. So what are you going to do about it?"

"Stop crying over him."

"Good for you!"

"And I *mean* it," Suz emphasized. "Life is too short for this BS. If he doesn't see how great I am, except tonight maybe, then I don't want anything to do with him." She paused. "He didn't see how bad I was tonight, right? He isn't here or anything?"

"Nope."

Suz slumped. "Oh, thank God."

"Ready to go?"

"Yes, but you're not coming." She was still slurring slightly, but she wasn't crying anymore and she was far more coherent than she'd been half an hour ago. "You're staying here. I have a good feeling about tonight for you. I want you to have some fun for once. I blew that for you tonight so far."

"No, you didn't," Noelle objected, but it was kind of hard to deny. It's never super fun to babysit a hammered friend.

Suz squinted at her phone and punched some buttons on the screen. Then she put it aside triumphantly and said,

"There. The cab is on the way." She looked at the phone again. "Five minutes."

"Let me at least walk you down to the street."

"That"—Suz hiccupped—"I will let you do."

The apartment was a third-floor walkup, and the walk down was long with a wobbly Suz. All the way, Noelle struggled with the feeling that she should be driving her, but what *was* the point? She lived about ten minutes' drive away, on the first floor, and on top of everything else she was insisting that Noelle stay at the party. She wasn't even welcome to take the opportunity to leave.

So when the cab arrived, Noelle checked out the driver—a woman, which put her mind at ease—and said good-bye to Suz.

Then she made her way back up to the apartment where the party was—whoever's it was—thinking about the guy in the kitchen all the way.

Honestly, she'd expected to run into him the moment she went in, but she didn't. In fact, she didn't see him at all, and her casual glancing around quickly turned almost frantic. She was headed back toward the kitchen when the gypsy fortune-teller called out to her. "You there, do you want your fortune told?"

Noelle hesitated. This was the kind of thing she'd normally refuse, but for heaven's sake, it was a party, it was just for fun. Why on earth not do it?

"I guess so." She sat down in front of the fortune-teller, a little uneasy. This was just a joke, right? What if she said something personal and other people heard it?

"Give me your hand." The woman held hers out and took Noelle's in a tight grasp. "Aaahhh, good, good. You have a long lifeline. Great happiness. And love. Mm-mmm, love. I see a tall man with very dark hair. Light eyes. He's closer than you think."

Self-consciously, Noelle glanced around.

"Do you know this man?" the woman asked.

"I . . . don't think so."

"His name begins with a *J*—I am not sure. Jacob. Jake. That's it. Jacob or Jake. He's very close. Very close." She released Noelle's hand and winked at her. "Good luck."

"Thanks," Noelle said, but it was more of a question than an expression of gratitude. Of course, it was just a party trick. She'd been hired to distract people, create some fun, but why be so specific.

"You're still here," a man said at her elbow, and she looked up to see him. The guy from the kitchen.

"Yeah. My friend went home. She . . . wasn't feeling too well."

"She wasn't looking too well. Holiday breakup?"

"You got it."

He shrugged. "It happens to the best of us."

"I guess so." She remembered tenth grade. She got a gold necklace from the guy anyway. Not a total bust.

"So the coffee, it was for her? Or are you a nervous wreck now?"

"Both." Noelle laughed, then lowered her voice. "To tell you the truth, I'm not even sure whose party this *is*."

"It's mine."

She gasped, horrified. "I'm so sorry!"

He laughed heartily. "Don't worry about it. It's actually my roommate's. I wanted to have an early night and go to sleep, but . . ." He gestured. "This."

"The perils of having a roommate."

"Indeed." He studied her for a moment. "You seem like a quiet type yourself."

"You're spot-on. I never go to parties."

He raised an eyebrow and looked at her with interest. "Then why did you stay?"

"Because I never go to parties. It's time for me to start doing things I never do."

"Do you ever kiss strangers?" he asked, taking a step toward her.

"Never," she said firmly, but something inside of her wavered and flip-flopped.

"Good policy."

"I know it."

"But there *are* times when it's absolutely appropriate."

"Oh yeah?"

He pointed up, and she followed his fingertip to a decorative little ball of mistletoe hanging over them.

"I see." But she wasn't sure about this. This was so far outside her realm.

"What's your name?" he asked.

"Noelle," she breathed.

"You're kidding."

"That's what everyone says this time of year."

He eyed her. "You look kind of familiar."

"Everyone says *that*, too," she said, but it wasn't true. He looked a little familiar, too, though she couldn't place him. It made her wonder if his familiarity was some sort of premonition.

"Well, Noelle, have you ever been kissed under mistletoe?"

"No."

He took her hand, pulled her ever so slightly closer, then, looking so deeply into her eyes that she was sure he could see her heart inside of her, raised her hand to his lips and kissed it. "Now you have."

"Oh." Everything in her relaxed. She hadn't realized how tense she'd been at the prospect until he let her off the hook. "That was very nice, thank you. Very unexpected."

He gave a laugh. "What can I say? I'm a gentleman."

"Thank you," she said sincerely. Then, "You didn't tell me your name!"

"Jacob. Jake. Jake Marsden."

She opened her mouth to exclaim in surprise, then

frowned. "Wait a minute, do you know the fortune-teller?"

"No," he said.

"But—"

"But I paid her five bucks to tell you that."

"You *did*?"

They both laughed. "I did," he said. "So if things don't work out, don't worry, you don't have to spend the rest of your life looking for another Jake because some gypsy told you about him."

"What a relief."

"Tell me, Noelle. Could I persuade you to go for a walk with me? All this noise and smoke is going to drive me nuts if I'm here much longer."

"I would love to," she said. "Jake."

Chapter 8

I t was the sound of the snowplow scraping by outside that jarred us both out of the moment.

"Zooterkins! What was that?"

I took the Manolos off, then got up and looked out the window to confirm. "They're starting to clear the streets. The snow has stopped coming down."

"Oh." She looked disappointed.

"It would be an utter nightmare if it just kept going and going and going and never stopped. Can you imagine? We might have been stuck here forever!"

"Oh, I don't think there was much danger of that. Where I come from, you can have snow whenever you want it. Or sun. Ocean or mountain. It's really quite lovely."

"It sounds like it." And in that moment I really and truly wanted to believe her.

In fact, in that moment, I really *did* believe her.

I can't say why. Certainly she wasn't all that persuasive herself, but she hadn't done a ton of talking. What made me question where she'd come from and why was the magical clarity of the memories she'd brought to me. Well, memories and . . . what would you call them? Memories that never happened? There should be a word for that, but if there is I don't know it.

"So do you remember anything about your life?" I asked her, deciding, for a moment, to go with her story.

She was keen enough to be onto me immediately. "You don't believe my 'story,'" she said. "Do you?" She raised an eyebrow.

I smiled and shrugged. "I might. A little bit. I have to say, I never heard anyone say 'Zooterkins' before, so you're certainly not from around these parts."

"I do apologize for cussing."

"Is that a cuss?"

Her face turned pink. "I mean it as one."

I laughed outright. "If that's not the definition of a cussword, I don't know what is!"

"He laughs when I say it, too." She jerked her head and eyes heavenward.

I laughed even harder. I didn't know who *he* was, whether it was God or some underling angel, but the idea of anyone up there in charge chuckling at this crazy old broad really tickled me.

"I believe you," I told her.

"You do?"

"I do." Maybe I was just giddy with the weird situation, but in that moment I genuinely did. "So what exactly are you supposed to do in order to declare *mission accomplished* on this night?"

"Oh, that's easy. You're supposed to spread your wings a little bit finally. It's time for you to stop chickening out of everything. *Especially* during the holidays. Do you realize that for the past eighteen years you have had one crummy holiday after the next?"

"Do I realize it?" I gave a dry laugh. "Yeah, I realize it." It wasn't as if they'd all been miserable, but there had never been a stellar one. And having been through the potential scenarios tonight, I could see that there could have been some really great ones, but I hadn't allowed for them. I'd been too scared of what could happen, when I should have been *excited* about what could happen.

"Then there is one more thing you need to consider," she said, and handed me a pair of Shoe Addicts Anonymous pumps. They were a gorgeous buttery soft black leather, cut low on the sides to give the illusion of a longer leg without going so far as to show the arch, and they were finished with a solid gold band around the heel. That was an SAA trademark. "Put these on."

"But we're almost finished—"

"Put them on!" she said, sounding what you might call cross, as I wasn't sure the woman had an *angry* bone in her body.

Assuming she had any bones at all, that is. Or any body. I guess if she was an angel, she wouldn't, right?

I put the shoes on.

✳

Noelle was working late, as usual—the week leading up to Christmas was madness—when her phone rang. She glanced down and picked it up.

"Hey, Lorna."

"Are you sitting down?"

"Almost always."

"Are you sitting down *now*?"

She laughed. "Yes, I'm sitting down. If you don't tell me what's up, though, I'm going to get up and start pacing."

"You're going to Rome!"

"What?"

"For *Christmas*! Well, *on* Christmas. Which kind of knocks out Christmas night, but who cares? You can't stand it anyway, so now you have a great excuse for being a grinch!"

"What are you *talking* about?"

"I have to go to Rome for the business, to pick out new designs, if you can even stand the idea, and Helene just bagged on me because her daughter has a Christmas pageant, so I'm going alone, except I'm *not* going alone, because *you* are coming with me!"

"I can't!"

"What do you mean you can't? You can. You will. I won't let you say no to such an awesome opportunity. We're going to stay in the Visconti Palace and walk the ancient streets every day, and drink strong Italian coffee with cannoli for breakfast—I don't care if it's dessert—and eat pizza and spaghetti and gnocchi and just loads and loads of things and we're going to get so fat." She gasped. "Oh my God, the prosecco! Imagine how much prosecco we can have! We can rent a Vespa like Gregory Peck and Audrey Hepburn in *Roman Holiday* and—"

"It sounds like you need to take your boyfriend, not me."

"Oh, shut up, you know guys don't ever want to do those girlie romantic things." She paused. "Wait a minute, why are you being so negative? I thought you'd be thrilled. This is like the opportunity of a lifetime. It's free," she added with a question in her voice.

"That's not the problem . . ."

"What's the problem, then? How could there possibly be a problem at all?"

Oh, it was so typical of Lorna. Everything was so easy for her. She got an idea and she followed it. She was the original Fantasy Island proprietor; everything was possible with her.

But it wasn't possible. Christmas was a week away, and there was no way Noelle could get herself together and ready to go abroad in that short time. Why, she'd have to tell Lex she was taking off work and . . . and . . . and get someone to collect her mail.

And a million other things. Just too many things to count.

"I can't do it," she said to Lorna. "I'm really sorry. I really do appreciate you inviting me. That is so sweet of you."

"Noelle," Lorna said in a stern voice. "This will be fun. And admittedly, I really would love to have you there. But honestly, I don't want you to come for *me* so much as I think you need to do it for *you*. When was the last time you were out of the country?"

Noelle thought about it. "Mexico."

"Mexico nine years ago Mexico? With me?"

God, had it really been that long? "That's the one."

"But there was a hurricane. And, wait, didn't you leave early, even?"

Yes. They'd been there two days when the weather report had come predicting bad weather, and while everyone else was content to hunker down in the hotel suite and live it up, Noelle had panicked at the idea of them all getting stranded there for weeks and had taken the last plane out.

To be fair, she had tried to persuade everyone to come with her. She didn't think it was safe there. But everyone else stayed, and to hear the stories, they'd had a marvelous time, even though Lorna herself had ended up having to pay an extra fifty bucks to get a second suitcase—full of new shoes—home on the plane.

"Noelle," Lorna said, her voice grave. "Please think about this. It's the opportunity of a lifetime. You can see the designs with me, help pick out next fall's line. It would be so much fun. For *both* of us. Please, Noelle. Get out of your cocoon for once."

The truth was, Noelle wanted to. Part of her could

envision it: taking her passport out of the little lockbox she had behind her Jane Austen collection on her bookshelf; packing a suitcase full of great shoes, black palazzo pants, sweaters, hats, sunglasses, everything she could think of to look stylish in Rome.

But she'd been through this kind of thing before; she had been disappointed before. She'd counted on things being one way only to find they went a completely different way over and over again. She'd begun to believe that gut feeling she got when she *knew* something wouldn't be a good time and she ended up being right.

Like that Christmas party she'd gone to a few years ago with Suz. She would much rather have stayed home, but instead she ended up having to escort her poor, drunk, heartbroken friend home and had ended up in bed, watching terrible TV by 11:00 P.M.

Two weeks later, Suz met the guy she ended up marrying—*not* the guy she'd been heartbroken over, by the way—but Noelle's life had remained the same, ever the same. Never changing.

It was just one example, and a small one at that, but she could come up with a hundred times she'd known something was going to suck and it did, from her high school boyfriend making New Year's Eve miserable to . . .

*

. . . to getting snowed in here tonight on Christmas Eve because I was too busy working to realize that, for other people, life had taken a turn.

For me, life never took a turn.

That's what Charlie's examples had taught me. That it *could* have but it never did. Because if there was such a thing as fate, could a person really screw it up that badly? That *consistently*? If there was fate and I was meant to experience it, wouldn't it have happened no matter what I said or did?

"No," Charlie's voice interrupted my thoughts.

"I beg your pardon?"

"I'm sorry to eavesdrop, I really am, we're only supposed to do it in extreme circumstances, but this is one of those. Your fate has come to you over and over again, and you have pushed it away."

"I haven't." Eavesdrop? She could hear my thoughts?

Charlie considered me. "Do you know the story about the drowning man and the boat?"

I frowned. "I don't know. I don't think so." This was crazy. Why were we suddenly talking about a drowning man and a boat? If she began to talk about *Titanic*, I was going to lose it.

"There was a man who was drowning," Charlie said. "And he prayed to God with all the faith in the world and asked him to save him. Well, then a boat came along and offered to help, but the man said, 'No, thank you, I'm waiting for God to save me.' This happened three times—three boats came before the man finally died."

"Great story."

Charlie laughed. "And when that man got to heaven, do you know what he said to God?"

"Nice robe?"

"He said, 'Why did you fail me? I thought you would save me, I had faith you would save me, but you let me drown!'"

I nodded, though I didn't quite get it. "I mean, I know this is a parable, but I don't know the point."

"The *point*, my dear, is that God said, 'I sent you three boats, and you refused them all!'" Charlie exploded into peals of laughter.

And I couldn't help it, I joined in. That kind of laugh is absolutely contagious. "Okay, okay, I get it. That's a good one."

"So God has been sending you boats all your life, child, but you never get out of your house long enough to get on one."

I got it. "You think I should go with Lorna on the trip to Rome in a few hours?"

"Why on earth not? You don't have so much as a goldfish to take care of, and I happened to see that pile of clothes you set aside in your little shopping expedition—"

I thought of my private-sale shopping at the beginning of the evening. "How did you know?"

"I saw it! I was trying to get in the whole time! I just kept getting caught and—oh, never mind. Grab yourself a suitcase from the luggage department and you're all ready to go."

I felt something stirring inside of me. Hope? Optimism? No. Better than that. It was *certainty.*

I was certain that I knew what I had to do.

"Can you excuse me a minute, Charlie?" I asked, then

went and found my phone and called Lorna. I didn't care that it was late.

Lorna's scream of joy upon hearing I would be joining her could probably have been heard all up and down Massachusetts Avenue.

Next I texted Lex to let him know what I was doing, expecting him to get the message in the morning. Instead there was an immediate ding as his answer scrolled across the screen:

Delighted to hear it! Get yourself a suitcase and whatever clothes you might need for your stay. Consider them a Christmas gift from me! Say hello to Lorna and company and please try to find yourself a nice Italian boy. I want to hear all the lurid details when you get back in the new year!

XOXO's from Lex

Finally, I went back to Charlie, but something was different. Charlie was wearing the little hat she'd dropped on her way in, but, more than that, something about her seemed to be . . . faded. The color of her clothes, the flush in her cheeks, all of it was muting as if she were disappearing.

"Charlie, what's happening?"

"Oh, nothing, dear. Nothing at all. I'm just so tired. Time for bed."

That was the truth. It was late, but I could catch a few hours before I had to go and meet Lorna at the airport.

We went back to the bedding department and our selected beds. This, believe it or not, felt like the craziest part of the evening to me. Getting into a model bed and sleeping in it. Pulling back the beautiful thick down comforter and sliding into the thousand-thread-count sheets. It was the coziest I've ever been.

Overhead, the holiday music played on, as it had all day and night, ushering in what was already the best—and weirdest—Christmas I'd had in decades.

From several yards away, I heard "Zooterkins!" and then a thump with what could only have been the accompanying flump of limbs.

"Charlie?" I called through the dim ambient light.

"It's all right, dear, I just have trouble getting into these blasted tall beds."

Elegant, I thought. They are *elegantly* tall beds. And we sold steps that led up to them because, yes, many people found them a bit challenging to get onto gracefully.

I had to try not to laugh. "Are you okay?" I asked her.

"Oh, yes, nothing can harm me now. It's just been so long since I had to get into a bed."

I wondered what she did instead of sleeping in a bed but opted not to ask, for fear the answer would be too long and go in too many crazy directions for me to follow. I needed sleep.

And after what seemed like no time at all, the heaviness of my exhaustion came over me like an extra blanket, sending me into a happy state of unconsciousness.

I don't know how much later it was when I woke to the loud scraping of the plows outside. There's always something a little sad, a little defeated, about that sound of plows at the end of the snow, indicating that the beautiful quiet flakes have stopped, the world is gathering into a nervous ball again, and it's time to get back to life, get back to work, get back on the streets and do your thing.

Part of me didn't want to. Not because I was wimping out on life or the trip, like Charlie might have said, but simply because this was the best Christmas Eve I'd had in ages and I wasn't ready to say good-bye to it yet. It would obviously never be replicated.

But I did wonder if I could stay in touch with Charlie. Crazy, silly, fun, kind Charlie. Could some sort of bizarre friendship come out of this? Could we get together for lunch now and then? Could I start having Christmas parties (Imagine! Me having a Christmas party!) and invite Charlie each year to reminisce about the time we were trapped in the department store?

"Charlie," I called, getting out of the delicious warm bed. "They're clearing the streets, and"—I looked toward the window to make sure—"it looks like the sun is starting to come up." I padded over toward the bed she'd chosen. "But I had this crazy idea, and I hope you—"

The bed was empty.

It looked like it had never been slept in.

"Charlie?" My eyes traveled to the floor at one side of the bed, then the other, as if I could see a Charlie-shaped hole in the ground where she'd fallen when she tried to get up, but of course there was nothing.

"Charlie?" I called again, louder, and started hurrying through the store, looking for her.

I looked at Filigree first, half expecting her to be there heating up a croissant or bagel and making coffee and tea, but it was empty and clean, exactly as we'd left it.

My next stop was the back room of the shoe department. She was probably there, working on picking up the rest of the shoes that had fallen when she came in. That made sense. She was considerate that way.

But no, the back room was perfectly clean, every box in place, nothing on the floor, no evidence that there had ever been any mishap whatsoever.

My pace quickened, not so much because I was worried about her—although I was—but because I was worried about me. Had I imagined the whole thing? How could she have disappeared without a trace, leaving everything in such perfect condition that there was no evidence of her at all? Even I would have trouble tidying up *that* much in such a short time.

So what had happened? Where was she? Where could she possibly be?

I searched the whole store, calling her name all the while, but couldn't find a thing. Not one piece of evidence of her. I must have looked for forty-five minutes. It was crazy. There was no reason for it at all. No logical explanation beyond . . . well, beyond the story she'd told.

There was no way that was true.

Was there?

"Noelle?"

Someone was calling me from inside the store.

"Hello?"

"Noelle!" There was some relief in the voice. "Where are you, dear?"

It wasn't Charlie, it was a man.

I moved toward the voice.

Chapter 9

I t was Lex.

"Oh, *there* you are!" He hurried toward me, scarf nearly falling from the shoulder of his camel's-hair coat. "I've been so *worried*."

"Worried? Why? I can't even imagine a nicer, or safer, place to be stuck."

"You were all alone in this big place, with no security guard!"

It seemed rude to laugh, but our security guard was another character from Central Casting, probably better at playing checkers in the park than apprehending bad guys.

"It was fine," I said, still a little disoriented by everything that had happened.

"Besides," he confessed, "I was more worried that you wouldn't have packed properly for Rome. Where's your suitcase?"

"I-I haven't—"

"I *knew* it!"

And he was right. "What time is it?"

"Nearly six," he said. "You poor thing, have you been up all night?"

I remembered the unmade bed on the display floor. "Actually no, I slept pretty well, but—"

"Did you at least get something to eat?"

"Oh, yes, Gemma led me through that, it was no problem, but—"

"Well, we have to get your act together for your trip to Italy, then, don't we? Thank goodness I made it on time."

I narrowed my eyes at him. "That's the real reason you hurried over here, isn't it? You thought I'd wimp out!"

"Yup!" He didn't even hesitate. "Now, did you at least pick out a suitcase?"

"No, but—"

"I knew it." He took me by the arm. He smelled of expensive cologne. It was wonderful. "Then we'll start there."

"Wait." I stopped. "There was someone else here."

He turned to me, alarm in his eyes. "Someone else is here?"

"Yes! Or no, actually, I think she's gone. I don't know." I frowned and looked around.

"She?" He seemed relieved. I guess he was imagining some gun-toting robber.

I tried to explain as fast as I could. "It was an older woman," I told him. "Maybe midseventies? I don't know, she could have been older, but she fell off the shoe shelves and—"

"Fell off the shoe shelves?"

"In the back room. She was trying to get her hat." I heard myself; I sounded nuts. I decided *not* to tell him about the weird time-travel hallucinations, for fear he'd have me committed. "That doesn't matter—the thing is, her name was Charlie and she was a little batty and she was here with me all night but when I woke up a little bit ago I went looking for her and I couldn't find her." I stopped. I *did* sound crazy. The whole thing had to be a dream. It had to be from the stress of being trapped. Unusual situation, a little scary not knowing when I'd be free—I probably fell asleep earlier than I'd realized and ended up having a wildly vivid dream. "Or, you know? Never mind. Now that I think of it, it was certainly just a dream."

He looked at me, thoughtful. "A dream. Hm."

"I just woke up!"

He nodded, though he still looked like something was behind his thoughts. "All right, then, let's do that shopping for your trip."

Relieved that he was letting the subject go, I said, "I think that sounds absolutely wonderful!"

He took me to the coat department first and picked out an elegant kimono-style black coat, midweight, with three-quarter-length sleeves that looked like something Audrey Hepburn might have worn. "This will be *perfect* in Rome this time of year!" he enthused.

Around the store we went, picking clothes, gloves, even a fascinator hat, which he *assured* me I could pull off and which would be absolutely wonderful in Italy.

Then to the shoes.

"You'll need these Jimmy Choos," he said, pulling the sample off the table. They were pointed-toe pumps with a wrap ankle and impossibly high heels, in a shimmery gold.

"I'll fall off those Jimmy Choos!"

"You'll learn to walk in them like every other stoic woman," he said, then laughed. "Italian men like a long, lean leg." He put his index finger to his chin and looked around. "The SJPs, of course." He picked the Minnie bootie with a zipper back, stacked chunk heel, and silver faux-snakeskin uppers. "Very stylish."

I'd never worn anything so stylish in my life. I tried to picture myself walking elegantly in them. I had a better chance in the SJPs than in the Choos, but I was ready and willing to take them all on.

"You'll also need some practical choices, of course. Naot?" He went to the table and picked a lovely black leather pair of open toe sandals you'd never know were comfortable because they were so cute. "You don't even need to break them in."

"Good, because there's no time."

We rushed around, picking items from here and there,

even a bottle of Miss Dior perfume, which Lex swore suited me exquisitely.

The pile of more practical clothes I'd already set aside at the beginning of last night was bagged and put in my office, none of it—according to Lex—suitable for my European excursion.

All of this was punctuated by calls from Lorna, telling me she'd gotten the ticket, then telling me we weren't able to sit together because it was too late to choose, but reassuring me the trip wouldn't take too long and my flying anxiety didn't need to come with me.

As I was about to drive to the airport—full of apprehension—Lex said, "You told me about a woman here with you last night. Charlie?"

"Yes." I felt embarrassed. "But she just disappeared. I don't know, Lex, maybe I was exhausted and had a long, vivid dream. But, boy, was it vivid."

"Can you tell me what she looked like?"

I sure could. "But I'm really not sure it wasn't just a dream."

"And I'm not sure it was."

"Okay . . ." I described her in great detail, adding the crazy hat at the end like icing on the cake.

"I know this sounds nutty," Lex said, "but she sounds exactly like Charlene Pennymar."

I thought for a moment. Why did that name sound familiar? Then it hit me. "The woman whose file you wanted me to find."

He nodded. "Every year about this time, I start wondering whatever happened to her. This year the curiosity really got to me."

"Why? Who *is* she?"

He gave a slightly self-conscious laugh. "She worked here some years ago and took on a job helping out with the holiday rush. It was a hard time; Mother had just died. Somehow Charlene knew all the right things to say and do, and even though she got a lot wrong—*boy*, did she get a lot wrong—she said she was here to help me, and she did." He looked off into the distance and nodded. "I never forgot her."

"Sounds like a godsend," I said, then realized that's *exactly* what Charlie had claimed to be.

He was quiet for a moment, then said, "She was a kind lady. Very grand. In the most unassuming way possible, that is."

Somehow that simple description seemed to sum her up for me. I continued to describe her, fascinated to find out if Charlie was indeed Charlene. I didn't tell him about my time-travel stories, though.

"That sounds just like her," he concluded. "And somehow it seems just like her to show up exactly when I was looking for her."

"Or when I was," I said softly.

He must not have heard me, because he said, "Were you able to get any information from her about where she might live now or how we could find her? I'd love to wish her happy holidays."

I shook my head. Should I really tell him she claimed to be my guardian angel? He'd think I was crazy. I didn't need him thinking I was cuckoo right after he'd helped me find all those glorious clothes and get packed for an overseas trip. So I simply said, "I suspect she came back to say hello to you and ended up locked in, like me. She was a little . . . dotty."

He smiled. "Like you?"

"Oh yes." I smiled back.

His smile faded slowly. "In all sincerity, I would have loved to see her again. She was a very special, cheerful lady. I always associate the holidays with her now."

"She could come back." I shrugged. "Keep an eye out for her. I have the feeling she shows up whenever she's needed."

✳

A few hours later I was making my way onto a crowded Boeing 747. I'd signed in late, thanks to buying my ticket late, so I was in the third and last seating group. Fortunately my carry-on was small, so I was able to fit it into the jammed overhead bin.

I sat down in the seat by the window—this always made me feel less claustrophobic while miraculously not triggering my fear of heights—and leaned my head against the wall, looking out at the airport workers loading luggage onto the plane and wondering if I was making a huge mistake by embarking on this journey.

The two seats next to me were mercifully empty,

though I had little hope they'd stay that way. It had been a lot of years since I was on a flight that wasn't packed full like a tin of sardines.

Lorna came over and sat on the edge of the end seat to talk to me, ready to jump in case the occupant showed up.

"So are you ready for Christmas in Italy?"

"There won't be much of Christmas left when we get there," I pointed out.

She frowned. "Okay, Captain Buzzkill, are you ready for *Boxing Day* in Italy?"

"Yes!" I laughed. I was. I was ready for anything in Italy. I didn't know where this newfound optimism came from, but I was going to enjoy it as long as I could.

"And New Year's Eve," she pointed out. "Don't forget, whoever you kiss at midnight, you'll be kissing for the rest of the year."

"I'm not seeing any big romance blossoming here suddenly," I said to her. "But thanks for the . . . warning?"

"Or promise." She shrugged. "It depends how you choose to look at it."

"Jury's still out."

Lorna laughed heartily. "I want you to know I don't

believe this Negative Nelly act for one second. You want to have fun; you're just afraid to. I guarantee you, you are going to have fun on this trip."

"Absolutely," I agreed heartily. "Don't worry, I know that."

"Good." She held her hand out for a high five.

I slapped my hand to hers. "This is going to be great. Thank you so much for talking me into it. Most people would have given up at the first no, because it's so ridiculous to say no to a glorious opportunity like this, but not you. Thank you."

"I knew you wanted to come." She winked.

The cabin bells tolled, and she stood up. "I'm going back to my seat, but it looks like you'll be alone. I'll come back when we're in the air."

"Great!"

I watched her make her way back to her seat and was beginning to wonder, giddily, at my luck in having the row to myself when I saw a man coming onto the plane and making his way down the aisle.

My heart sank. There was no way he was going to go past me; virtually every other row was at least two-thirds full.

Sure enough, he stopped at my row and opened the overhead compartment, somehow shoving his carry-on in.

My purse vibrated, and I realized I hadn't put my phone on airplane mode. That was weird. I could have sworn I did. Nevertheless, it was dinging. I didn't want to be the jerk interfering with airline/tower signals, so I opened my purse and took out my phone, but it was off after all. I puzzled over that for a moment and couldn't think of anything else in there that could be causing the problem.

As I put my phone back, though, I noticed a loose piece of paper in my bag. That hadn't been in there before. What was it?

I pulled it out and it was weird—it seemed like old paper, a little browned at the edges, like something that had been written a long, long time ago.

But when I opened it, I could see it was definitely to me.

Noelle,

Enjoy your trip to Italy. I think you will find that you made exactly the right choice. Have a wonderful time, dear.

Especially on the flight.

With Love, Charlie

The man was about to sit down when he stopped, pulled off his coat and hoodie, and shoved them—*somehow*—into the overhead compartment as well.

That's when I recognized him.

It was *him*.

Here he was again, entering my life unexpectedly, when I was finally taking the road not taken. At least my own road not taken. I'd seen it over and over again with Charlie.

He sat down next to me and smiled. "Looks like we might have a free seat on our row."

I nodded, breathless, speechless at the sight of him.

He must have picked up on it, because he looked at me and cocked his head. "Do I know you?"

"I think . . ." I cleared my throat. "No, not really, but . . . I think we might have gone to high school together . . ."